Without warning he seized her in his arms...

'Mr Tenby—'

One hand still held her while the other slid its way up her arm. Then he released her.

'Get out of that damned uniform and wear something civilised,' he ordered.

'Very well, sir.'

'"Very well, sir,"' he echoed. 'Such a cool voice. Such a *neutral* voice. God, I wish I could see your face this minute.'

'It's a neutral face too,' she assured him. 'Just treat me as a piece of machinery.'

'There's machinery in my factory. It smells of axle grease, not wild flowers, as you do.'

Elinor was startled. 'I came up because I'm not happy about you having too many people in here just now,' she said quickly. 'You still need a lot of rest and I—'

'No, I think you should listen while I make a few things plain,' he interrupted her. 'I've been ill as long as I can afford to be. So if I want to talk to my manager I'll do so. You'll do what I say, when I say, and that's final. Now go before I start getting angry.'

Lucy Gordon cut her writing teeth on magazine journalism, interviewing many of the world's most interesting men, including Warren Beatty, Richard Chamberlain, Roger Moore, Sir Alec Guinness, and Sir John Gielgud. She also camped out with lions in Africa, and had many other unusual experiences which have often provided the background for her books.

She is married to a Venetian, whom she met while on holiday in Venice. They got engaged within two days, and have now been married for twenty-five years. They live in the Midlands, with their three dogs.

One of her books, HIS BROTHER'S CHILD, won the Romance Writers of America RITA award in 1998, in the Best Traditional Romance category.

Recent titles by the same author:

TYCOON FOR HIRE
RICO'S SECRET CHILD

TAMING
JASON

BY
LUCY GORDON

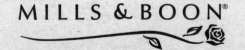

MILLS & BOON®

MILLS & BOON and MILLS & BOON with the Rose Device are registered trademarks of the publisher.

First published in Great Britain 1999
Harlequin Mills & Boon Limited,
Eton House, 18-24 Paradise Road, Richmond, Surrey TW9 1SR

© Lucy Gordon 1999

ISBN 0 263 81935 3

Set in Times Roman 10½ on 12 pt.
02-0002-48739 C1

Printed and bound in Spain
by Litografia Rosés, S.A., Barcelona

PROLOGUE

SHE wouldn't cry. No matter how desperately she longed to, she wouldn't cry and let the hated Jason Tenby know how badly he'd hurt her.

Cindy Smith pressed her hands against her mouth to force back the sobs. Through the blur of tears she could see the countryside flashing past the car. With each mile she was moving further away from the man she loved.

Jason Tenby sat beside her, his eyes fixed on the road. He never once glanced her way and she knew he was indifferent to her broken heart.

There was power in every line of him, from the arrogant set of his head to the way his hands rested on the wheel, controlling it with the lightest of touches.

For him, control was everything. It had maddened him that his younger brother, Simon, had chosen a girl from the wrong side of the tracks to marry into the proud Tenby family. So he'd set himself to smash the engagement. And he'd done so with brutal efficiency.

Although he was still in his late twenties his face had an authority that he'd inherited. Generations of Tenbys had lived at Tenby Manor, ruling the surrounding countryside, either openly or through subtle influence. Jason Tenby was the last of a long line of masters.

The girl sitting beside him was no match for him. She was eighteen, with fine bones and a delicate, vulnerable face. In her short life she'd known poverty but not harshness, and her first brush with implacable force had left her devastated.

5

'We'll reach the station in five minutes,' Jason said. 'Plenty of time for you to catch your train.'

'You've no right to do this,' she said wildly.

'We've been through all that.' His voice sounded bored and impatient. 'It wouldn't have worked. Take my word for it, Simon wasn't the husband for you.'

'Because he's a Tenby, and my mother used to scrub floors for you,' she said accusingly.

'Look, don't—'

'You decided to break us up as soon as Simon introduced me, didn't you?'

'More or less, yes. But don't make a tragedy out of this. You're eighteen. Your heart will mend fast enough.'

'It's so easy for you!' she cried. 'You give your orders and everyone else has to fall in line. But I didn't, did I? I wouldn't take your money or listen to your hints about how I didn't fit in—'

'I was only trying—'

'So when you couldn't break me any other way you— you—' Suddenly her control broke. 'Oh, God, how could you do it?' she sobbed. 'How could you be so cruel?'

'We've arrived,' he said, halting the car. 'Don't make a scene in public. I know what you think of me, and it doesn't matter.'

'Nothing matters to you but getting rid of me.'

'I'll certainly be happier when I've seen you onto that train.'

When the train pulled in he shoved her bag inside, and urged her in after it.

'Don't cry, little girl,' he said in a gentler voice. 'And try not to hate me. Believe me, this is best.' He slammed the door.

The guard blew his whistle. Quickly Cindy pulled down

the window and leaned out, looking right into his harsh face.

'But I do hate you,' she choked. 'I hate you because you trample over people and don't care about their feelings. You got rid of me because you thought I wasn't good enough. Well, I'm going to prove you wrong, and then I'm coming back.'

'Don't come back,' he said harshly. 'Stay right away from this family.'

The train was beginning to move.

'Do you hear?' she called. 'One day I'll come back.'

He didn't try to answer, but stood looking after her until the last moment. She thought she saw a look of surprise on his face.

She'd sworn to return, but only out of pride. How could she ever go back to the place from which she'd been so cruelly ejected?

And yet it happened.

Six years later Nurse Elinor Lucinda Smith returned to Tenby Manor as the last hope of her enemy, Jason Tenby, who was lying blind, crippled and alone.

CHAPTER ONE

IT WAS dark in the room, and very quiet. The man in the bed lay in the mute blackness of despair.

Nurse Smith watched him for a moment before saying, 'Good afternoon, Mr Tenby.'

Silence. He might have been dead.

His eyes were covered, as they had been ever since the accident that had almost killed him. Elinor knew how bad the injuries beneath those bandages were. She looked at his hands lying on the coverlet. Such big, ruthless hands, like the man himself. Jason Tenby had enforced his will on all who crossed his path, but today he was helpless, at the mercy of a woman who called him her enemy.

Elinor Smith pulled herself together. She was a nurse, sworn to protect the sick and vulnerable, and this man was both. It didn't matter that he'd smashed her love and condemned her to a lonely wilderness. It was her job to care for him.

'I don't want any more damned nurses,' the man said tiredly.

'I know. They told me at the agency.'

'The last two ran away.'

'You mean they stormed out in indignation.'

Jason Tenby gave a grunt. 'You've heard about that too?'

'The head of the agency told me everything. He said it was fairer to warn me about you.'

'So you've only yourself to blame for ignoring his warning.'

8

'That's right. I've only myself to blame.'

'How long, I wonder, before you storm out?'

'It'll take more than you can throw at me.' She was feeling her way, sensing that a robust approach would work best with this patient. Sympathy would merely drive him crazy. He was already on the edge of endurance, clinging on with frantic fingertips to a crumbling sanity.

She looked around his old-fashioned room, with its big oak bed and heavy oak furniture. The carpet was a deep brown, and russet curtains hung at the tall windows.

It was an intensely masculine room with nothing soft or gentle about it. The man who lived in this wealthy house spent little on his personal needs. A hard man. A comfortless man in a comfortless desert.

'And your name?' he asked at last.

'Nurse Smith.'

'I meant your first name.'

'I think Nurse Smith is best for the moment.'

'The formal approach, huh?'

'It'll make it easier for you to yell at me.'

'I guess it will at that. Tell me what you look like.'

'I wear a white uniform and a white cap. And black, sensible shoes.'

In the long pause that followed, she could sense him sizing her up.

'By God, you're a cool one!' he said at last.

'I'm here to help you, Mr Tenby. That's all that matters. I want to see you up and walking, as you used to.'

His voice had a bitter edge. 'And you really think that can happen? Have you read the notes?'

'Yes. There was a fire in your stables. You went in to rescue a horse and the roof fell on you.'

Another grunt. 'Damned horse wasn't even there. Someone else had already got it out.'

'It must have been hard having all this happen for nothing,' Elinor agreed. 'You were lucky not to have been seriously burned.'

'Yes, people keep telling me how lucky I was,' said the sightless figure on the bed.

'You were partially protected by the beams that fell on you. Because of them your burns were superficial, and have now healed. So have your ribs. Your back's injured and your sight has been damaged, but with luck that won't last.'

'You're just giving me the same line they all do. But you don't believe it either.'

It was true. She was nowhere near convinced that he would see or walk again. But he had to be convinced of it if he were to have a chance.

'I believe it can happen if we work at it together,' she said firmly. 'And that's what we're going to do.'

Suddenly his brows drew together and he covered his bandaged eyes with his hand. Elinor could see that something vital inside him had cracked.

'For God's sake, go!' he said in a shaking voice. 'Just leave me.'

'Certainly.' She closed the door firmly so that he could hear that she'd gone.

Mrs Hadwick, the housekeeper, was waiting in the corridor.

'All your bags have been taken upstairs, miss,' she said. 'I'll show you the way.'

Because she was on edge over her meeting with Jason, Elinor had chosen to visit him first, before even going to her room. Now she followed the housekeeper down the corridor and round the corner. And, with alarm, she realised where she was going.

'This room—' she said.

'It's the best guest room,' Mrs Hadwick said, pushing open a door. 'I'll send you up some tea.' She vanished.

The room was big and imposing, with a four poster bed in the centre. There was a dressing table, an ordinary table and chair, and a big, comfortable armchair. There were two tall windows with drapes that swept the floor. Nothing had changed since the last time she'd slept here, six years ago.

Until now she'd managed to control her memories, but in this place they came flooding back.

Simon seemed to be with her, young and handsome, full of love and eagerness, as he'd been the day he first brought her to his home as his future bride, driving with one arm around her shoulders, and one on the wheel of his gleaming new sports car. They'd swept up the long avenue of oaks until suddenly the house had come into view, and she'd gasped at its beauty and splendour.

'Simon, I never dreamed—that can't be your home?'

'What's the matter with it?'

'I've never been in a place like that before. I grew up in one of those shabby little back-to-back places at the town end. My mother was a cleaner in your father's factory.'

He gave a shout of laughter. 'No, really? Tell me.'

'She used to do the early morning shift. One day she took me with her. It was against the rules, but otherwise I'd have had to stay at home in an empty house. We nearly got away with it, but one morning I bumped into your brother.'

'Jason? You mean you've already met? Suppose he remembers you?'

'I was eight years old. He won't know me after all these years. You mustn't tell him. Promise.'

'I promise.'

'Cross your heart and hope to die. Oh, dear, I wish now I hadn't told you.'

'Darling, that really hurts me. If you can't trust me, who can you trust?'

'Oh, I didn't mean that. Truly I didn't. Of course I trust you, but don't you see? I don't belong here.'

'You belong with me,' he said firmly.

How desperately she loved him. It seemed as if her slender form must shatter with the force of her love.

As they neared the house she saw a tall man standing on the steps. He'd been a teenager when she'd glimpsed him in the factory, but she had no trouble recognising him again as Jason Tenby.

He must have been a good six foot two, with broad shoulders and a certain massiveness about his presence that had more to do with his air than his build. His hair was dark brown with a touch of red, and his skin was tanned as though he spent a lot of time outdoors. He wore riding breeches and a tweed jacket and stood at his ease, one foot on the lowest step, his hands thrust into his breeches pocket. He looked for all the world like a patriarch watching the hordes advancing on his domain, sizing up a threat.

'How do you do, Miss Smith?' His voice was deep and vibrant. Had she imagined it contained a sneer, as though he was mocking her for her commonplace name?

His very handshake was unnerving. Her delicate hand was swallowed up in his great fist, and she almost gasped from the strength of his grip and the sense of power that came from him.

She remembered every moment of her first evening at Tenby Manor. It was the first time she'd been in a house where people dressed for dinner. At least, she thought, she could live up to her surroundings, for she had an expensive long gown and a delicate sapphire pendant, both of them Simon's gifts. He was wonderfully handsome in dinner jacket and black tie, although even her adoring eyes could see that he was cast into the shadow by his brother.

Simon was twenty, slim and mercurial, with fair, boyish looks and rapid speech. Jason was twenty-eight with slow, thoughtful speech and an authority beyond his years.

Simon enchanted her. Jason awed her.

There was only a slight brotherly likeness between them. Already Jason's face was harsh with experience, and there was a firmness about his mouth and chin that revealed his impatience with fools, or with anyone who disagreed with him. Yet when in repose his mouth had an unexpected curve, suggesting humour, sensuality, even charm. She grew nervous whenever he looked at her because his dark eyes seemed to swallow light, and it was impossible to read his thoughts in them.

The walls of the grand dining room were lined with portraits of Tenby ancestors, and under their censorious eyes she was sure she would use the wrong knife and fork, or knock over one of the lead-crystal glasses. But it wasn't as bad as she'd feared. Jason talked to her cordially enough, and showed no sign of recognising her from years ago. Afterwards he showed her around the grand house, and they sat talking in the library.

'So, how did you meet my brother?' he asked, handing her a sherry.

'Hasn't Simon told you?'

'I'd like to hear your version. He has a tendency to— shall we say—embellish things?'

She nodded. 'He does have a wonderful imagination,' she agreed eagerly. To his dour brother Simon's tendency to get carried away might be maddening, but after her dull life it was a glorious plus.

'Wonderful,' Jason echoed. Then, unexpectedly, he grinned. She couldn't help herself smiling back, and for a moment a flash of understanding passed between them.

'I was working in a shoe shop,' she said with a touch of defiance. 'And Simon came in to buy some shoes.'

He'd stayed two hours and left with five pairs—'because I couldn't tear myself away from your sweet face', he'd said over dinner that night.

'Have you done any other kind of work?' Jason asked.

'I was going to train as a nurse, but my mother became ill and I stayed at home to look after her until she died.'

'And you didn't start your training then?'

'Well—then I met Simon,' she said, and nothing could have stopped the gentle smile that crept over her face.

She heard a sound like a sharp intake of breath and looked up quickly to find Jason staring at her, hard-eyed.

'What does your father do?' he demanded abruptly.

'He's been dead for ten years.'

Joe Smith had fallen into a ditch while weaving his drunken way home from the pub, gone to sleep in a foot of water and never woken again. She could imagine what this stern man would make of such a story.

She noticed Jason frowning as she spoke, and suddenly he leaned towards her and said, 'You really are Brenda Smith's daughter. I couldn't believe it at first—'

So he'd recognised her after all, she thought in despair.

'Yes, I—that is—'

'And we met that day in the factory. Well, well! A little more sherry?'

While she was sipping he suddenly demanded, 'What made you choose that dress?'

Taken off guard, she did what came naturally to her, and replied with complete honesty. 'Simon chose it.'

'So I would have supposed,' he replied dryly. 'Paid for it too, I dare say.'

'I didn't ask him to—'

'Don't say a word. I know my brother. That thing is much too old and sophisticated for you.'

'I—I thought it would be suitable,' she stammered.

'You mean you thought you should dress up and pretend to be something you're not. Damned idiotic idea! Who do you think you're fooling?'

Her cheeks flamed. He saw it and added more kindly, 'Don't take it to heart. I'm a plain man—a rough man, some would say—and I talk plainly. And, in plain words, you and Simon are a mistake.'

'You can't tell that in one evening.'

'I could tell it in one minute.'

To her relief Simon came looking for them then. Jason said no more, but let Simon take her away for a stroll in the garden.

'He knows me,' she said, distraught. 'He recognised me all the time. It's not funny—' Simon had broken into a chuckle.

'I'm sorry, darling,' he choked. 'What did he actually say?'

'He said, "You really are Brenda Smith's daughter. I couldn't believe it at first—". Oh, Simon, don't you see what that means? He saw it during dinner and he kept it to himself until he was ready.'

'Did he tell you what made him realise?' Simon asked in a curious voice.

'No. Oh, what does that matter? He was laughing at me all that time.'

'He enjoys being one up on people,' Simon agreed

'What else did he say?'

'Isn't that enough? He despises me because I haven't got any ''background.'''

His laugh came echoing down the years to her now. How young and delightful he'd been! How generous and full of charm! 'Who cares about background?'

Her name was Elinor Lucinda, but Simon called her Cindy. Cindy for Lucinda, but also—

'Cindy for Cinderella,' he teased. 'My little Cinderella.'

Her poverty enchanted him. 'I love giving you things,' he said that first night as they walked under the trees. 'I'm going to cover you with diamonds.'

'But I don't want diamonds. Just your love, my darling. Nothing but your love.'

'You can have that as well, all tied up with a big shiny bow, and anything else you ask for.'

Lost in delight, she hardly realised that they'd returned to the house and were crossing the hall. Only then did she see Jason, standing on the stairs, close enough to hear Simon's extravagant promises. But her own voice was softer, and Jason had probably missed her gentle protest.

She had a brief glimpse of his face, dark and angry, before he turned away.

Jason never mentioned what he'd overheard, but in a dozen ways he made it clear that Simon was dependent on him for money. Simon confirmed it.

'I inherit plenty under my father's will, but Jason's got the purse-strings until I'm twenty-five,' he said with a shrug. 'So what? How can he stop me using my credit cards? And when the money is spent, how can he refuse to pay up? It's my money, after all. Don't worry about it.'

That was his philosophy of life. Don't worry about it.

And somehow things always worked out Simon's way. Living under his spell, as she did, it was easy to believe they always would.

She guessed it was no accident that their bedrooms were at opposite ends of the great house. In fact Jason's precautions were needless. The young girl hadn't yet offered herself totally to the man she adored, and she loved Simon more for respecting her wishes. The day would come soon when they would be one in flesh as they were one in heart and soul. But just for now she was enjoying this sweet time of anticipation.

So Jason's resolve to keep his brother out of her bed was an insult. He couldn't have said more clearly that he saw her as a schemer. And at last she heard those words from his own lips. She came across the brothers by accident, and couldn't help overhearing Jason's voice.

'You young fool. You're not going anywhere near her room if I have to bar the way myself... The last thing I want is that girl getting pregnant...'

She fled before they could discover her. She would have liked to flee Tenby Manor altogether, but there was a strong inner core beneath her gentle exterior, and it made her determined to stay and fight for her love. Yes, even to fight Jason Tenby himself. And she knew he was a formidable foe.

'Why don't you chuck Simon back into the sea?' Jason asked once. 'You'll find other fish that suit you better.'

'I'll never love anyone but Simon,' she said fervently.

'Then you're a fool.'

'And Simon? Is he a fool?' she asked, more bravely than she felt.

'Yes, because he believes in the same kind of love that you do. I've seen his infatuations before. He enjoys the romantic stage, putting the girl on a pedestal, buying her gifts, asking for nothing back.'

He said the last words with a sneer that stung her into retorting, 'I can't imagine you asking for nothing back.'

'Then you're a good judge of character,' he said with a raffish grin. 'The romantic bit is all very nice, but I'm the one who has to pick up the pieces, sort out the broken hearts, the whole boring thing.'

'But you've got it all wrong,' she said passionately. 'I understand why you're concerned for your brother, but I won't break his heart—'

'Only his bank account, eh?'

'That's a wicked thing to say—'

'Look, I've seen some of the presents he's given you— all bought with money he doesn't have.'

'I don't ask him to—'

'Sure you don't. You don't need to. He enjoys splashing out. Well, I can be generous too—for a purpose.' He named a sum of money.

'Are you trying to buy me off?' she demanded, outraged.

He shrugged. 'Put it how you like. It's a good bargain.'

'And my-self respect? How would I buy that back?'

'That's a good line. I'll up the offer a little, but not much.'

'You could double it and I still wouldn't be interested.'

'No, don't overplay your hand. I won't double it.'

Furiously she stormed off, but at the last minute something made her turn back to look at him, standing there, regarding her with a sceptical look.

She was used to waking early, and she enjoyed getting up with the dawn to look out of her window and watch the sun rising over the Tenby estate. At such moments she could forget the tensions that swirled around her, spoiling this beautiful place.

But then one morning it was spoilt anyway, by the sight of Jason pounding up the avenue of oaks, mounted on Damon, his big black stallion. Simon had called the horse 'a ferocious brute who tries to kill everyone who comes near him', but Jason sat him as easily as if he were a pony.

He wore no jacket, and through his thin shirt she could see the tension of his muscles, controlling the huge beast without effort.

He thought he could control everything, she thought—his estates, his brother, the whole world. But she wouldn't let him control her.

A moment later he stopped under her window.

'Do you ride?' he called up.

'I—yes,' she said.

'Good. I'll find you a mount.'

She'd made a bad mistake. Her mother had once done housework for a man who owned a fat, elderly pony. He'd let the child play with the animal, and she'd learned to saddle him and sit there while he ambled slowly about. And she'd thought that was riding.

She looked good in a riding habit that belonged to their recently married sister, but almost at once she knew she'd done something stupid. Her mount was gentle enough, but it was a real horse. It needed to be properly ridden. And she didn't know how.

What happened next would always fill her with shame.

The horse simply ignored her, going happily on its own way, while she grew more and more miserable and humiliated. Her one real effort to take charge resulted in the beast trotting off to the nearest stream and stopping so suddenly that she was deposited in the water.

It was Jason who hauled her out. 'Why did you pretend you could ride?' he demanded, exasperated. 'Of all the idiots!'

'I can ride, but not on an animal like that,' she insisted, pulling off her sodden jacket. Beneath it she wore a thin white sweater, which was also soaking.

'What do you mean, ''an animal like that''?' he yelled back. 'It's a horse, for Pete's sake. It's got one leg at each corner and nothing between its ears: It's a mount for a child, always assuming the child knows what it's doing. What did you learn on, a rocking horse?'

'Stop it!' she cried. 'Stop trying to bully me.'

'Bully you, you stupid girl? I'm trying to prevent you making the biggest mistake of your life.' Suddenly he seemed to lose his temper, taking hard hold of her shoulders. 'Stop trying to be something that you're not, d'you hear? Get out of here while you can. Simon isn't the man for you.'

'That's for me to say. Simon loves me and I love him.'

He gave her an exasperated little shake. She tried to pull free but he held her harder than ever. 'Love,' he said contemptuously. 'What do you know?'

They held each other's eyes, both now equally furious. She could hardly believe her own anger. Normally she was sweet tempered to a fault, but suddenly all the restraints were off and a fierce emotion rose in her, sweeping all before it, startling her. It startled her enemy too. She could see that in his eyes, as though something unexpected had winded him.

'Hey!'

Simon's voice surprised them both. He'd ridden up while they were preoccupied. Jason swore under his breath and released her. Simon threw himself down from

his horse and put his jacket around her. Jason remounted
and galloped off without a backward glance.

That evening Simon carved their initials on the oak tree,
kissed her, and said, 'I could have knocked him down for
holding you like that. Did you know you were almost
naked from the water?'

She blushed and laughed. 'You don't need to be jealous
of your brother. He's the last man I could ever look at. I
can't see how any woman could even like him.'

'Jason knows how to make himself pleasant when it
suits him. But when he wants to make himself unpleasant—look out!'

'And he wants to make himself unpleasant now,' she
murmured. 'But it won't make any difference to us, will
it?'

'We won't let it,' he assured her.

How blindly confident she'd been that Simon could
cope with every problem! How pitifully naive that confidence seemed now! Jason had managed to part them
because he'd sworn to do so, and his will was inflexible.

But how could she ever have imagined that he would
do so in a way so cruel, so callous, so unspeakably
wicked?

Looking around the luxurious bedroom, Elinor knew she
was mad to have returned here where bitter memories
mocked her at every turn. She'd refused the job at first,
and it had gone to someone else. But two days ago the
other nurse had suffered a family crisis. The head of the
agency had pleaded with her to fill the gap, and she'd
decided perhaps it was time to confront her ghosts.

The first face to greet her hadn't been a ghost. Mrs
Hadwick had worked for the Tenbys all her life, but she'd
been away for Elinor's first visit.

Her decision not to tell Jason who she was had been an impulse. Smith was such a common name that he couldn't identify her from that alone. Even Elinor wouldn't mean anything to him. He'd known her as Cindy.

She'd done it for his sake. Telling him the truth would only put pressure on him, and he had enough pressures already.

She too was feeling pressured. She'd vowed to return, and she'd done so, in defiance of Jason's order to 'stay right away from this family'.

Now it didn't feel right. She'd made that vow in grief and passion, but over the years all passion had drained away from her, replaced by the will to make something of herself. She'd worked night and day to qualify as a nurse.

She'd had no social life. She wanted nothing more to do with love. While other girls dated she'd studied, and passed her examinations near the top of her class.

These days she was a poised, elegant professional woman. There was nothing to connect her with the awkward girl who'd last come to Tenby Manor.

Or so she'd thought, until she'd seen her enemy again.

Time had gone back and she'd relived their first meeting, holding Simon's hand for reassurance. Then she'd remembered that she was Nurse Smith, highly qualified and much in demand. And Jason Tenby was a sightless wreck of a man, who needed her help if he was ever to be anything else.

The knowledge brought her no satisfaction, only a weary conviction that she'd assumed a burden too heavy for her.

Then she pushed the feeling firmly away. She'd learned to be strong for herself. Now she would be strong for her patient. That was all he was. Just a patient.

CHAPTER TWO

WHEN the door had closed behind Nurse Smith, Jason Tenby lay in the darkness, straining to listen. His body ached with tension, his head was thumping and the very silence seemed to sing in his ears.

He wished he could force himself to relax, but he'd never known how. From the moment of his birth he'd been the Tenby heir, carrying the burdens of Tenby expectations. His father had died when he was twenty-two, leaving an inheritance of death duties that had fallen like a lead weight onto his shoulders.

He'd broadened them to bear the load. The family traditions made him personally responsible for every worker on the land and in the factory. It was his job to ensure that there would always be work for them.

Jason had never shirked an obligation in his life.

He'd paid off the debts and made the property more prosperous than ever before, but it had taken its toll on him. He hadn't consciously renounced pleasure, but he'd deferred it to some indefinite future, and now he hardly remembered it.

'Don't let any man—and certainly no woman—see that he knows more than you,' his father had barked. 'You're the top man. Nobody must get the better of you.'

Over the years he'd learned the value of that advice. And he'd added 'Never let the world know you're afraid'. There had been a lot of fear. Fear of not being up to the job, fear of people *suspecting* that he wasn't up to the job.

But nothing had prepared him for the fear that lived with him now. It stalked him in the daytime darkness. It waited to pounce when he slept.

It filled the void of his life. Fear of the nightmares. Fear of the future, of people he could hear but not see, of medical staff because they knew more than he did.

Nurses came and went, driven off by his bitter rage. But today there had come one who wouldn't yield. He'd sensed it in her manner, heard it in her quiet voice. She was strong and confident, and she would fight him back.

Soon his factory manager would arrive to make his twice weekly report and receive Jason's instructions. He tried to clear his mind so that he could appear to be in command. He mustn't think of what might wait for him: years of being blind and crippled. Because then the fear would rise up and engulf him.

'Mrs Hadwick—'

'Call me Hilda, love.'

'Thank you, Hilda. And I'm Elinor.' She gave her friendliest smile. 'I'm sorry to be a nuisance, but could you find me somewhere else to sleep? I need to be near my patient at night.'

'There's a room right opposite his,' the housekeeper said doubtfully. 'But it's just a cupboard.'

It turned out to be very small, with barely enough space for a bed, a chair and a wardrobe.

'I'll be fine,' Elinor said. 'What matters is to be where he needs me.'

Hilda regarded her with approval. 'None of the others thought of that. They were only too glad to get away from him. He's not the easiest patient.'

'No, I gathered that.'

'When it first happened, I thought he'd go crazy. He's always been such an active man, and suddenly he couldn't see or move. It'll be terrible if—' She broke off as if she couldn't bear to speak the thought.

'You're very fond of him, aren't you?' Elinor said, surprised. It was hard to picture anyone fond of Jason Tenby.

'Oh, yes,' Hilda said at once. 'He's been very good to my Alf and me. When Alf lost his job Jason found him work on the estate. That's Jason for you. He looks after his own.'

Elinor didn't answer this. She had reason to know how Jason Tenby looked after his own.

As they made up the bed together Hilda gossiped about the family.

'Not many of them left now,' she said regretfully. 'Only Jason, his brother Simon, and their sister. She married and went to Australia. Simon lived here until a couple of years ago. He's in London now.'

Elinor had known that Simon had left because the last nurse who'd held this job had given her a rough briefing. It was a relief to know that she needn't fear meeting him.

How bitter his face had been at their parting. How terrible were the names he'd called her. It wasn't his fault. Jason had forced the situation on them. But Simon had believed the worst of her so easily. How could he?

She pulled herself together and asked some bright, meaningless question. Hilda answered it and the moment passed.

'But with any luck there'll soon be a family again,' she chattered on. 'We're all looking forward to the day Jason brings his bride home. Just as soon as he's well, he'll marry Miss Virginia.'

'Not Virginia Cavenham?' Elinor said before she could think.

'Yes? Do you know her?'

'No, but ·I've heard the name Cavenham.' The Cavenhams were a notable local family. Elinor hadn't met Virginia, but she'd heard her called the pride of the crop. Simon had spoken of her as a future bride for Jason even then. She was 'suitable'.

'The families have been friends for years and we always knew Jason would probably marry one of the two girls,' Hilda said now.

'Suppose he hadn't wanted to?' Elinor asked curiously.

'Then he could have had Jean Hebden, or one of the Ainsworths,' said Hilda, naming local wealthy, land owning families.

'But suppose he wants to look beyond the Cavenhams, the Hebdens or the Ainsworths?'

'Land marries land,' Hilda said firmly. 'Or money. That's how great old families survive for centuries.'

When Hilda had gone Elinor looked about her, struck by how easily her meagre possessions fitted into the cramped space. There were a few clothes, a change of uniform, something for 'best', some sweaters, a couple of pairs of jeans. Her underwear was white and functional without a flower or a piece of lace to be seen.

Her make-up told the same story: enough to wear when necessary. Nothing elaborate. Her books barely filled the shelf: a few detective stories for lighter moments, but mostly medical works. She liked to keep abreast of the latest advances.

Of course she could explain this austerity. She travelled light. She'd never been fond of accumulating possessions. There were always plenty of reasons.

But in her heart she knew it wasn't much to sum up a life. A withered life. A withered heart. She resisted the thought, but she couldn't entirely deny it.

The mirror inside the wardrobe door showed her a neat, efficient young woman, her face unadorned, with a hint of tension about the mouth. The beginnings of frown lines between the eyes told of long nights of study, days filled with work, years without a holiday, without feelings, without anything.

Yet her skin still had the peachy bloom of youth. Her features were regular, her mouth wide and shapely, with something that might have been sensuality still lurking in the corners. If her face had been animated it would have been beautiful. If her large blue eyes had glowed with love or laughter she would have been irresistible.

But love and laughter had died long ago.

The memories came in swift, dazzling pictures now, and she was forcing herself, like a rider ramming an unwilling horse at a jump. With every step the horse tried to retreat, knowing that what lay ahead was misery and horror. But the rider drove it on.

The dinner party in her honour. Simon crowing that Jason had given in, silencing her instinctive knowledge that Jason would never give in. Puzzled. Fearful. Wondering what Jason was planning.

On the day of the party, a team of caterers arrived and started preparing the dining room, carrying in baskets of food and wine. In the midst of the bustle the two brothers withdrew to Jason's study and had a furious row from which each emerged set-faced and grim.

'It's nothing, darling,' Simon said when she asked. 'Just Jason throwing his weight around. Forget him. Go and make yourself look beautiful for tonight.'

But there was something preoccupied about his manner that worried her. Several times that day she caught him looking at her in a thoughtful way.

The twenty guests all smiled and greeted her with interest but with little half glances at Jason, as if curious as to what he was thinking. She, too, wondered what there was behind his smile. In the midst of festivity she felt her apprehension growing.

After dinner someone sat down at the piano and there was an impromptu dance. She danced with Simon, to applause.

Then Jason stepped forward and held out his arms, inviting her. Only it was more command than invitation.

She was surprised at how skilfully he danced. It would have been a pleasure to partner him if she hadn't been so much on edge.

'Smile,' he said. 'This is your night of triumph.'

'I don't feel triumphant,' she assured him gravely. 'Only happy. I really do love Simon. If only you could believe that.'

Unexpectedly he said, 'I find it all too easy to believe. I only wish I didn't.'

'Then if you believe me—'

'Has it ever occurred to you that Simon isn't the man you think him?'

Enlightenment dawned, and a smile broke over her face. She felt filled with sudden light.

'What is it?' he demanded sharply. 'Why do you look like that?'

'Because now I understand what's really bothering you?'

'Really!' he said ironically. 'Then it's time we had a talk.'

He steered her towards an open door, and led her into the library.

The pictures flickered as Elinor flinched back from what came next. She didn't want to remember. Leave it there. Surely there was no need to relive the pain?

But some perverse imp of memory forced her to look again, and watch herself go into the library with Jason. She saw not only their two figures, but her own foolish confidence that at last she'd got the better of this ruthless man. She wanted to reach out and snatch that silly little innocent away from the danger she was heading into so blithely. But nothing could do that now.

In the library they faced each other.

'So tell me about this wonderful insight that's come to you,' he said ironically.

'I've just realised—you know Simon's dark side, don't you?'

He was startled. 'So you do recognise that he has a dark side?'

'Of course. Everyone has.' A growing confidence made her add, 'You certainly have.'

Instead of being offended he gave his wolfish grin, and said, 'Go on. I can't wait for the next bit.'

'All right, I don't know his dark side. But then, he doesn't know mine.'

'Your what?'

'Oh, I do have one,' she said, laughing. 'I'm terribly grumpy in the mornings. I can't imagine Simon ever being grumpy, but I'm prepared to find that I'm wrong. When you really love somebody, you love everything about them—even their faults, because those faults are part of them.'

And so she went blundering on, reciting the confident

words, playing into his hands, watching the derision on his face, not understanding it.

As well as scornful, he was furiously angry. 'You think you know it all!'

'I know about love, Jason. I love Simon and he loves me, and nothing will ever part us. We'll stand by each other through the worst that you can do.'

As she grew more exalted she smiled up into his face. He drew in his breath and his brow darkened.

'You simpleton!' he grated. 'You baby! You stupid, pretty little idiot! You naive, gullible— Heaven give me patience!'

He gripped her shoulders, looking at her intently. Suddenly they heard Simon's voice outside in the hall. She saw the tension come swiftly into Jason's face as though he'd made a lightning decision, and the next moment he pulled her hard against him, sliding his arms about her body, lowering his head and crushing her mouth with his own.

Abruptly the pictures flickered out into blackness.

Time and again her memory stopped at this point, and only resumed several moments later, with the sight of Simon's face, white and distraught.

'You cheating little bitch,' he cried. 'You scheming, deceitful— All this time I thought you loved me, but you had your eyes on a bigger prize, didn't you? I trusted you!'

She tried to protest, but he cut her short. 'I loved you. I'd have given my life for you, and the moment my back's turned you go straight into my brother's arms. What else have the two of you been up to?'

'*Nothing,*' she screamed. 'Simon, *please*—it's not what you think.'

'It seemed clear enough to me. Oh, God, Cindy, how could you do this?'

All the guests seemed to be there behind him, listening to his heartbroken accusations, witnessing her shame.

'Listen to me,' she begged through her sobs.

'Listen to you! I never want to listen to or even think of you again. Get out of my sight.'

'That's enough!' Jason intervened. 'You've made your point, Simon. Now leave it. It's over.'

'Yes, it's over,' he choked. 'Over, Cindy, *over*! And I thought you and I were for ever.'

He turned and fled upstairs. She followed him, but found his door locked against her, and her frantic hammering produced no response. At last she slid to the floor, sobbing in despair.

She didn't know how long she stayed there, but eventually Jason came to tell her that all the guests were gone.

She looked up at him through eyes blurred with tears.

'You—you did this on purpose,' she choked.

'Yes, I did it on purpose. Come on, get up.'

He put his hands under her arms and hauled her firmly to her feet. She went with him because there was nothing else to do. She had nobody but Simon, and now he'd turned against her.

Jason led her to her room, and said curtly, 'Pack your things. You're leaving in the morning.'

She clung to the hope that she could see Simon before she had to leave, but in the early hours she heard a car start up beneath her window. She ran and opened it, and was just in time to see Simon drive away.

He'd gone out of her life for ever, disillusioned, believing that she'd betrayed their love.

But the true betrayal had come from his brother, who

had forcibly kissed her, knowing that Simon was about to come in and see them. Why, oh, why couldn't Simon understand that? Why had he believed the worst of her so easily?

Jason insisted on driving her to the railway station. She left behind every gift, every last tiny piece of jewellery that Simon had ever given her.

But she left behind much more than that: youth and dreams, hope, love, and a belief that the world was good. She'd been brutally robbed of them all.

As she stood now, looking at her own tense, sad face in the wardrobe mirror, she understood for the first time how totally these things had been drained from her, and how empty was the woman they had left behind.

She shut the door abruptly and went downstairs.

The kitchen had changed since she was last here. The old one had been a monument to antiquity. The new one paid lip-service to tradition, with oak beams on the ceiling and copper pans on the wall. But the gadgets were modern, as Hilda demonstrated with pride.

'I had to talk him into it,' she said, pointing at the ceiling to indicate Jason. 'He likes the old ways, and the old values. But I told him, this kitchen may have been good enough to cook for Queen Victoria, but it ain't good enough for me.'

'Did Queen Victoria ever visit Tenby Manor?' Elinor asked.

'So they say. Wouldn't surprise me. Anyway, I put up with it as long as I could, then I said, Either that ancient kitchen goes, or I do.'

'And what did Mr Tenby say to that?'

'He said, ''Hilda, Tenby Manor would go to pieces

without you.'' And there was a man in here, taking measurements, the very next day.'

Elinor was surprised. Even discounting the story's more colourful details, the bottom line was that Jason Tenby had listened to Hilda. But of course, by modernising, he'd improved the value of the house.

The outer door, which had been slightly ajar, was pushed open and a muddy black spaniel scampered into the room.

'Bob, you rascal,' Hilda called, 'where have you been hiding?' She offered a titbit, which the spaniel pounced on. 'He's Jason's. Nobody's got much time for him now, poor little thing, so he spends his life wandering around the grounds.'

'Mr Tenby's? He didn't—' Elinor checked herself on the verge of saying that Jason hadn't had a dog when she was last here, and substituted, 'He didn't seem the kind of man to keep a pet.'

'He's more than just a pet. He wins prizes at all the dog shows. Pedigree as long as your arm. Not that he looks it now, because he's covered in mud. But he's actually Lord Robertson Winstanley Mooreswell of Hatley Place,' Hilda pronounced triumphantly, adding as an afterthought, 'The eighth.'

I can believe that, Elinor thought. Even this man's dog has a pedigree.

Bob bounded towards her.

'Stay away from me!' she said sharply. Then she coloured and added, 'His paws—'

'Yes, you don't want them on your nice clean uniform,' Hilda said.

Elinor agreed, but not without a touch of shame. For a moment her hostility to all things Tenby had extended to the innocent animal who'd been welcomed because he had the pedigree she herself had lacked.

To cover the moment she began to ask about the house. 'It's a big place to manage on your own.'

'I'm not exactly on my own. I clean Jason's room because he doesn't like strangers in there, but, for the rest, a couple of cleaning women come in from the village. My Alf does odd jobs and looks after the kitchen garden.'

She concentrated on the supper she was preparing, and told Elinor that it would be ready in an hour.

'Meat and two veg, with plenty of gravy,' she announced with pride. 'I do it for him every day. And a good solid pudding for afters. If only he did more than pick at it! Never mind. I'll build him up.'

Elinor forbore to comment that Hilda wouldn't build Jason up by cooking meals that obviously didn't tempt him. The time wasn't right.

From outside she could hear someone coming down the stairs, leaving the house and driving away.

'That'll be the factory manager,' Hilda said. 'He's been getting his orders.'

'You mean he's been up with Mr Tenby?' Elinor asked, startled.

'He comes here twice a week. Dr Harper—that's Jason's GP—tried to stop him, but Jason got into such a fury he had to back down.'

'I think I'd better have a word with Mr Tenby.'

She found Jason lying still and silent. It was hard to tell if he was awake or not.

'What are you staring at me for?' he demanded irritably.

'I'm sorry, I didn't think I was.'

'I knew you were. Don't you realise that's one of the

worst things? People who stare at you, thinking you won't know. People who think being blind is the same as being stupid.'

'Mr Tenby, I don't want you to think of yourself as blind—'

'Sure! Fine!' he snapped. 'I'm not blind, it's just that I can't see anything.'

'For the moment. It may not be permanent, and it's better if you don't get into a "blind" state of mind.'

He gave a snort. 'You nurses should get your act together. The last one told me exactly the opposite; never stopped twittering on about adjusting to reality.'

'Adjusting to reality before you're certain that it *is* reality is just giving in,' Elinor said calmly.

There was a silence.

'So you can talk sense about something,' Jason grunted.

'You'd be amazed at the things I can talk sense about,' Elinor told him crisply.

'Good. You can stay here for the moment. But there's one thing.'

'Yes?'

Without warning he reached up and gripped her arms in both hands.

'Mr Tenby—'

'Keep still,' he rasped.

One hand still held her while the other slid its way up her arm to the throat of her uniform. Then he released her.

'Get out of that damned uniform and wear something civilised,' he ordered. 'You make me ill just standing there in it.'

'Very well, sir.'

'"Very well, sir,"' he echoed. 'Such a cool, calm, collected voice. Such a *neutral* voice. God, I wish I could see your face this minute.'

'It's a neutral face too,' she assured him. 'Just treat me as a piece of machinery.'

'There's machinery in my factory. It smells of axle grease, not wild flowers, as you do.'

Elinor was startled. She wore no perfume and used unscented soap. What had he detected that was hidden from the rest of the world?

'I came up because I'm not happy about you having too many people in here just now,' she said quickly. 'You still need a lot of rest and I think we should—'

'No, I think you should listen while I make a few things plain,' he interrupted her. 'I've been ill as long as I can afford to be. There's work to be done and nobody I can trust to do it. So if I want to talk to my manager or my bailiff I'll do so. I hope that's clearly understood.'

'Perfectly. If you think you're sufficiently on top of your work to give orders about it, I have nothing to say.'

'Don't try to get clever with me!' he snapped. 'You're my nurse, not my keeper. I will not be molly coddled.'

'I'm delighted to hear it.'

'So why does Hilda tell me you've moved in across the corridor? If that's not molly coddling me, what is?'

'That's a matter for my professional judgement. While you're still in a bad condition I prefer to be near you at night.'

'The hell with that! You move right out of that room and back into the other one. Do you hear?'

'I hear. But I'm staying put.'

'Then I'll tell Hilda to move your stuff.'

'You'll do no such thing. Hilda has enough to do without becoming pig-in-the-middle between us. You want a fight? Fine! We'll fight. But leave Hilda out of it.'

He ground his teeth. 'I think fate must have it in for me! It's not enough that I'm laid out here, useless to myself and everyone else. I have to be cursed with a harpy who marches in here giving orders like some prison commandant. I'm still the master here, in case you didn't realise it.'

'I should think the whole world realises it if you shout like that,' Elinor observed mildly.

'I shout because it's the only way I can get myself listened to. You'll do what I say, when I say, and that's final. Now clear out of here before I start getting angry.'

CHAPTER THREE

BEFORE Elinor could reply there was a clattering in the corridor outside then a knock on the door.

'Got your supper,' Hilda called.

As she wheeled the trolley in Jason turned his head in her direction and Elinor noticed that he made the effort of a smile.

'What good care of me you take, Hilda! Why should I need any other nurse?'

Hilda's plain face flushed with pleasure, but she said, 'You stop your nonsense now, and do what the nurse tells you.'

'All right, all right!'

'Shall I set it up for you?' Hilda began to make her way to an invalid table by the window. It had a free end, designed to swing over the bed.

'No, Nurse Smith will do it,' Jason told her. 'Thank you, Hilda.'

The light faded from his face as the door closed behind her. The pretence of cheerfulness had drained him.

'The table's over there somewhere,' he said.

'Shall I help you sit up?'

'*No*—yes, dammit!'

She slipped an arm under his shoulders, and he gripped her other arm. It was an effort not to flinch, remembering the last time his hands had grasped her, but she stayed calm, although her heart was beating fast. Gently she eased him into a sitting position and pulled more pillows

up behind him. Then she laid out the meal on the trolley
and swung it over the bed.

'What is it?' he demanded, sensing her hesitation.

'Hilda's left you a jug of gravy, Mr Tenby, but do you
really want it?' She chose her words carefully. She'd
nursed the blind before, and knew how they hated gravy
because it ended up everywhere.

Jason grew still and there was a sudden arrested look
on his face as though he'd heard, unexpectedly, the one
hint of understanding he'd been listening for.

'No, I don't,' he admitted at last. 'Hilda's a dear, but
she doesn't think.'

'Is there anything else I can do for you?'

'If you mean do I need my food cut up, no.'

'Then I'll leave you.'

'Yes, go and start moving out of that room.'

She left without answering. In her own room she
changed out of her uniform but made no attempt to move
her things.

Downstairs, Hilda had a meal ready for her. She'd laid
a table in the dining room, evidently feeling that Elinor's
dignity demanded this. But after one meal in solitary state
Elinor decided to eat with Hilda in the kitchen. She carried her plates through, and began to help with the wash-
ing-up.

'By the way, I looked in to see how he was managing,'
Hilda said, 'and he told me to move your stuff.'

'No,' Elinor said urgently.

'Don't you worry. I listened with my deaf ear.'

'Which ear is that?'

'It varies,' Hilda said mysteriously. 'You do it your
way.'

Elinor laughed. She already liked Hilda very much.

When she returned to Jason his first words were, 'Have you got rid of that uniform?'

'Yes, I'm in ordinary clothes now,' she assured him.

'Let me feel.' He held out his hand commandingly.

'Why don't you just take my word for it, Mr Tenby?'

'Because I can't take anyone's word for anything,' he shouted.

After a jagged silence he added, 'I'm sorry. When you're in the dark—there's only mistrust—I don't know how to explain—'

'You don't need to,' she said at once. 'It was my fault. I should have been more understanding. Here—' She took his hand and guided it to her arm so that he could feel the soft texture of her sweater. He touched her only briefly before withdrawing his hand.

'Thank you,' he said distantly. 'There was no need for that. Of course I believe you.'

He'd eaten little. Some of the food had fallen onto the sheet. She tidied it up quietly, removed the tray and wheeled the table away from the bed.

'I'm going away to study my predecessor's notes,' she said. 'Tomorrow we'll discuss your treatment.'

She was afraid that he might mention her room again, but he made no reply and she left quickly.

It was good to be alone. So far the day had shaken her more than she wanted to admit. She went downstairs and out for some fresh air.

There was a stiff breeze that set the daffodils dancing. Elinor pulled her coat about her and headed into the wind. She would confront the last of her ghosts, and drive them away, she reasoned.

But the ghosts were wicked and mischievous, lying in wait around every corner. There was Simon, a smiling boy, his arms open to her. And there, running to him, was the most painful ghost of all—her own younger self, brimming over with happiness.

Suddenly she pulled up short and pressed her hand over her mouth to stop the anguish welling out. She leaned against an oak tree, clutching it for support while memory shook her. It might all have been so different.

After a while she drew a long breath, lifted her chin and walked on.

It had been high summer when she'd come here last, and the season had reflected the joyous flowering of love in her heart. Now it was late March, the moment when winter turned into spring. The trees were still bare, although a close look would have shown the buds ready to burst into fresh life, but she didn't see them. For her, spring had never come again.

The big house stood on a hill, looking out over the grounds and beyond them the valley, as though the Tenbys must keep everything beneath their watchful eyes. A beautiful building of honey coloured stone, with elegant proportions, it had been built three hundred years ago by a Tenby with money to spare. Down in the valley was the town of Hampton Tenby, dominated by Tenby & Son, an engineering factory that was the largest employer for miles.

The Tenby family motto was *Beware the Lion's Roar*, and it had perfectly summed up their power. Now it seemed even more fitting for Jason—a lion whose wounds had made him dangerous.

The wind was getting up again and the light was fading fast. The feeble sunset turned the windows to gold. Blind eyes, staring out over the countryside. Elinor shivered.

Six years of not allowing herself to feel anything had left her unprepared for the conflicting emotions that tore at her now.

Jason Tenby had destroyed her. If she'd wanted revenge she could have had it today in the sight of his
misery. But she wasn't vengeful, merely cold and tired,
and wishing with all her heart that she'd never come back
to this place.

By the time she'd finished making him comfortable for
the night Jason looked exhausted. His face was drawn,
and there was a tense look about his mouth that made her
ask, 'Are you in pain?'

'Not physically. It's just the thought of the night. For
God's sake give me something to make me sleep.'

'Your last nurse seems to have let you rely on sleeping
pills rather a lot.'

'Maybe she understood more than you do what it's like
to be trapped.'

'Trapped?'

'In the darkness—and silence. Sometimes I listen to the
radio, but after a while it's just another way of being
trapped.'

'I'll give you something tonight,' Elinor said, 'and
we'll talk about it tomorrow.'

She gave him his usual pill and tried to settle him more
comfortably, but he fended her off.

'Goodnight,' he said curtly.

'Goodnight, Mr Tenby.'

It was too soon for her to go to bed, so she went down
to the kitchen and spent an hour chatting with Hilda over
a pot of tea. When she finally went upstairs she paused
outside Jason's room and listened, shocked by the sounds
coming from inside. He was groaning and muttering like
a tormented soul. She stood, undecided, for a long time
before quietly entering.

He'd told her to leave the curtains pulled back, and the

moonlight poured in onto the bed, revealing how he lay still for a moment, then resumed the feverish tossing.

Elinor crossed quietly to the bed, wondering if she ought to awaken him from whatever agonies overwhelmed him in the night.

But she guessed that this was why he'd tried to banish her from the room opposite. He didn't want her near enough to hear his nightmares, and it would revolt his pride to know that she'd been in here.

'Why—why—?' The words came from Jason in a hoarse whisper.

'Mr Tenby—' She came closer, wondering if he'd awoken.

Suddenly he gave a violent lurch and one flailing arm caught her on the side of the head. But he went on tossing, and didn't seem to know what he'd done, or that she was there. So it seemed as though he was still asleep.

She caught his arm and held it gently. 'It's all right,' she said, reciting the words she'd used before in similar situations. 'Everything's going to be all right. I'm here.'

'Where?' he cried hoarsely.

'Right here, beside you. Feel me.' She caught his other hand, guided it to her, then let him hold her arms. He was muttering again.

'What is it?' she asked, putting her face close to his and whispering, trying to get through to his tormented brain without waking him.

'You're not real,' he groaned.

'Yes, I'm real, and I'm here to help you.'

'You're never real—always a dream in the end—'

'Not this time,' she said, wondering who he was talking about.

'Tried to make it right—but I could never find you—'

'There's plenty of time to make it right,' she assured him.

'Too late—you vanished—'

'You can tell me one day soon,' Elinor told him gently.

He was lying still now, although his breathing was tortured and sweat stood out on his brow. She mopped it with a handkerchief that lay beside the bed, and the gesture seemed to calm him, although he still held onto her as if his life depended on it.

'Don't go,' he murmured.

'No, I won't go, not while you need me.'

He reached out for her, finding his way up her arms to her neck, her face, stroking the hair that tumbled about his hands. The feel of it seemed to take him aback for he paused, wreathing his fingers in the soft locks, frowning.

Elinor took a sharp breath and drew away. Nursing him was one thing, but this kind of intimacy with her enemy wasn't in the bargain. Slowly, trembling, she took hold of his hand, meaning to free her hair. But his hand was so thin, so lacking in strength, that she couldn't bring herself to make a sudden movement.

He released her hair, but his fingers moved on, drifting across her face. She grew very tense as he reached the wide curve of her lips. There he stopped and lingered, as if caught in some spell. She held still, aghast at the sensations that his fingertips were sending through her.

They were warm, sweet feelings, delicious and forbidden. Her heart beat madly and she couldn't breathe.

Suddenly a terrible fear possessed her. She didn't know why she was afraid of this man who was virtually helpless, but the fear came out of nowhere, shaking her like a rag doll. It was connected with something she couldn't remember—*wouldn't* remember—and it left her shivering with shock. She must get out of here, now, this minute, but his tortured face seemed to hold her.

'*Why did you go?*' he whispered.

Scarcely knowing what she said, she replied, 'I had to go. You know why.'

What had made her say that? The words had seemed to come of their own accord, but she'd known they were the right ones.

He sighed. 'Yes, I know why. But if I could only—I wanted to—I tried—but it was too late. Don't you see—*it was too late*?'

Without warning his clasp tightened, drawing her closer. Before she could stop him he'd pulled her right down, so that her lips were on his. She stiffened against him, while her mind rebelled with horror.

And with anger, too. Even now, while he was sick and sleeping, Jason Tenby simply took what he wanted, so deep rooted was his instinct to command, to possess.

'Let me go,' she insisted fiercely, struggling to free herself.

'No—' he whispered against her mouth. 'You mustn't go again. You might vanish back into the dark, and I couldn't bear that. Stay with me—don't condemn me to despair.'

She didn't know how to answer. His words were mad, senseless. Yet they found a mysterious echo in her heart, and that was the most senseless thing of all. He wasn't demanding now, but begging, and she couldn't sustain her anger in the face of that anguished plea.

He kissed her again and suddenly she had no more strength to resist. Thoughts and feelings rioted together. She must stop this—it was unprofessional—he might wake—she must get away—how warm his lips were—how seductively they moved against hers, enticing her response. How sweet the feelings that surged up—how joyful, wicked, terrifying.

Her own mouth began to caress his. It was madness but she couldn't help herself. The world might come to an end but she was held, helpless, in a timeless magic that made a mockery of propriety, and even of hostility. In that other dimension there were no friends or enemies, only lovers.

And then it was all over. His hands slid back on the bed as though the strength had suddenly drained out of them, and she was free to go.

The abrupt ending of the magic was almost as shocking as its beginning. Her heart was pounding and shivers—whether hot or cold she couldn't have said—still possessed her body. But for him it had ended.

Moving slowly, so as not to disturb him, Elinor rose and backed away from the bed. Jason lay like a man stunned. His breathing was quiet and relaxed, and she knew that he was sleeping normally at last.

She escaped to her own room. There she stood in the darkness, shaking with the terror of what had happened to her. And yet nothing had happened. Her patient had been in distress and she had comforted him. That was all. She must cling to that thought. She *must*.

She awoke to the sound of a March wind blustering and sobbing around the house. Rain lashed the windows and the sight that met her eyes when she looked out was depressing.

She wondered what would happen when she went into Jason's room. How deeply asleep had he been last night?

Would he remember anything?

She found him lying quite still in an attitude of tension that told her he was awake.

'Good morning,' she said quietly. 'Did you sleep well, Mr Tenby?'

The question was a coded message, telling him that she hadn't heard his disturbance. Some of the tension went out of him.

'Excellently, thank you.'

'The weather isn't very nice,' she said conversationally. 'I expect you can hear the rain.'

The words meant nothing. She was establishing the territory, saying anything except what was really in her mind.

Who were you talking to in your dream last night?

It couldn't possibly have been Cindy Smith. Could it?

Behind her she heard a pattering of feet in the corridor and a soft yelp. She turned in time to see Bob dash into the room.

'No!' she said, aghast at the state of him, for he'd been out in the rain. Before she could stop him he came bounding across the floor, long ears flapping, and took a flying leap onto the bed.

Jason gave a soft grunt as Bob landed on him. The next moment his arms were about the dog, offering his face to the animal's frantic licks. For the first time Elinor saw him smile with real pleasure.

'There's a boy,' he was saying. 'Good boy, good boy.'

He embraced the frantically wriggling little body, and Bob went mad with delight. Elinor regarded him, fascinated. Jason's face was alive with warmth and love, making him a different man.

'Hey, you're going to be in trouble,' he said, feeling the muddy coat. 'I guess the bed's a mess, Nurse?'

'That's putting it mildly. Never mind. It's not the end of the world.'

'You must have left the door open. Normally I don't allow him in.'

'But why not? I can see he adores you.'

'It's no place for him, shut in with my moods—'

'You might be in a better mood if you had more of his company. And it's exactly the right place for him. He's trying to tell you that he's not just here to be played with. He's here to console you as well. That's his job, and you're denying him the chance to do it.'

'It'll make extra work for you.'

'It doesn't matter. Sheets and pyjamas can be washed. I'll get you a clean jacket right now.'

'And you don't mind?'

'I've got a job to do as well, Mr Tenby, and I want all the help Bob can give me.'

He lay back, fondling the dog's ears. 'That's not what the last one said.'

'Let's consider Bob part of the nursing team. But you, you mucky pup—' she patted the dog's head '—are under my orders now. Next time you let me dry you off first.'

'Hear that?' Jason asked the dog. 'You've got to do as you're told.' He added wryly, 'I guess we both have.'

Elinor shooed the dog away for his breakfast. 'And I'll bring yours when you're shaved and presentable,' she told Jason.

She pulled off the muddy top sheet, and helped him off with his pyjama jacket. An ugly scar disfigured his chest from the emergency operation that had only just saved his lungs from being pierced by broken ribs. Now Elinor could clearly see the shape of those ribs through the skin.

The broad outline of his chest was still there, but it had a wasted look. He was a lot thinner, and she could understand why Hilda wanted to build him up.

It struck her suddenly how alone he was in this house,

with only paid employees to care for him. Where was his brother, his fiancée? Where was anyone who loved him?

Of course, he'd driven them off, just as he'd tried to drive her away. But suddenly it seemed terrible that, at this time of his agony, he was in the hands of a woman who hadn't even wanted to look after him.

'Where do I find your clean things?' she asked.

'In the drawers at the left of the window.'

She found the jacket and handed it to him. He gave a grunt of thanks and made a small defensive movement, as though afraid she would try to put it on him. But she left him to do it himself while she went for a sheet.

When she'd finished making up the bed he said, 'You can't go on calling me Mr Tenby. Jason will do.'

'Very well, Jason.'

'And I want to know your first name.'

'Elinor,' she said. 'Now I'll get your breakfast.'

'My estate manager is coming this morning,' he said firmly.

'Then you'd better eat plenty to be at your best for him.'

When the manager arrived an hour later Elinor left the house for a walk. The rain had stopped and a watery sun had come out. Everywhere the trees were hung with droplets of water that caught the light and gave the scene a magical appearance.

But she saw none of it. Her eyes were turned inwards to a woman who'd come here reluctantly to nurse a man she hated, and betrayed every nursing standard she lived by on the very first night.

She hated him, but she'd let him pull her into his arms for a forbidden kiss that had given her exquisite pleasure. She could have—should have—tried harder to resist. But she hadn't—for the patient's sake, of course. To have struggled would have been to risk him waking and finding himself in an embarrassing situation. The patient must be protected at all costs.

That would do for now. But sooner or later she would have to face the real reason. And it would mean opening a door in her mind that she'd kept bolted and barred for six years.

She walked for a couple of hours, until at last the manager's car passed her in the lane that ran through a wood, driving away. She headed back and was nearing the house when she felt a soft thrumming in the earth beneath her feet, followed by the sound of hoofbeats. She turned and saw a chestnut horse, ridden by a beautiful young woman, coming straight for her from the other side of a fallen tree. The rider's tall figure was grace personified as she crouched low over her mount's back for him to take the jump.

She landed close to Elinor, who'd backed hastily, spattered her with mud, and rode on into the distance without a glance. Elinor indignantly brushed herself down, wondering who the rider was who cared so little for the rest of the world.

She found Jason tired. She took his temperature, and discovered that it was up. But she made no comment, not wanting to irritate him.

'What's that?' he demanded. His sharp ears had detected the crunch of gravel beneath his window.

Elinor looked out. 'It's a young woman on horseback. She passed me in the grounds.'

'Virginia,' he said.

Elinor just had time to tidy the bed before the door was flung open and a vision of elegance burst into the room.

Lady Virginia Cavenham was thirty, with a haughty

beauty and the kind of assurance that came from being born into wealth and privilege. Her jodhpurs revealed long, shaply legs, her riding jacket looked couture, and around her neck she wore a white scarf of pure silk. Her face was made up too heavily for the country, and a musky perfume seemed to waft into the room ahead of her.

'My darling,' she cooed, flinging wide her arms to Jason, who couldn't see them. The next moment she leaned over the bed and enveloped him in a scented embrace.

'Well, you took your time getting back,' he said good humouredly.

'Darling, I know I'm a few days overdue, but London is so crowded. Everything took longer than I thought, and I had to drop in on all the gang. Simply everyone asked about you.'

'That was kind of them.'

'They're all too, too devastated by what's happened, but they were just thrilled when I told them how splendidly you're getting on.'

'I'm glad you told them that.' Jason's voice was touched with strain, but Elinor was sure Virginia would be oblivious.

Her impression of the young woman was deeply unfavourable. Virginia seemed to have no sensitivity to how things would seem to the sick man.

Virginia's next words confirmed it. 'Did you get my card?'

'Yes, Hilda read it to me,' Jason said.

'It took me ages to find the right one.' She seemed to become aware of Elinor in the room and gave a ripple of laughter. 'Oh, heavens, not again. Jason, darling, you haven't sent yet another nurse screaming into the night?'

He managed a grin. ''Fraid so. This is her replacement, Nurse Smith.'

Virginia rose and approached Elinor, hand outstretched, beaming a smile at her.

'Smith,' she bubbled. 'What a wonderfully bland name for a nurse.'

'It has its uses,' Elinor agreed, refusing to be provoked.

'I think you're a perfect saint to look after my poor Jason. None of his nurses can stand him for a moment. I do hope he's paying you pots of money.'

'I get the regulation payment,' Elinor said coolly.

'Well, you'll soon be demanding danger money. You have all my sympathy.'

She was plainly putting herself out to overwhelm Elinor with charm. Elinor remained firmly underwhelmed.

'You're very kind,' she said, politely.

Virginia regarded her askance, as though she'd expected her overtures to be met with more enthusiasm, and was offended that they weren't.

'Haven't I seen you somewhere before?' she asked.

'You nearly rode me down,' Elinor said, adding significantly, 'That was nearly an hour ago.'

On horseback Virginia should have reached the house well before her. That she hadn't suggested that she'd enjoyed a leisurely ride before visiting her fiancé.

But it took more than that to disconcert Lady Virginia Cavenham. 'Yes, I love this place so much I just had to take a look around on my way here,' she gushed. 'I could murder a coffee. Hilda knows how I like it made. And some for Jason.'

'None for me,' Jason said quickly.

'Darling, of course you must.' She glanced at Elinor. 'Hurry please.'

Elinor returned a few minutes later with a tray, which she set down by the bed.

'You haven't brought any for Jason,' Virginia complained.

'Mr Tenby said he didn't want any,' Elinor reminded her.

'And I asked you to bring some,' Virginia said crisply.

'Miss Cavenham,' Elinor said quietly, 'Mr Tenby is my patient and my employer. I take my orders from him.'

She left the room without another word. She was very cross.

CHAPTER FOUR

DOWNSTAIRS was a small conservatory which Elinor had taken over. It had more space than her bedroom, and with glass on two sides she had all the light she needed to work.

Elinor noted down Jason's temperature plus the time, and generally brought all her notes up to date. After a while she saw Virginia's horse being brought around to the front door. The next moment Virginia came into the conservatory. She had recovered her good humour.

'Jason says you're doing a marvellous job, so I expect he'll be up and about soon.'

'I don't know about soon,' Elinor said cautiously. 'His injuries were fairly severe.'

'But he'll be able to see again, won't he?'

'I have every hope.'

'He's a very important man around here. A lot of things would simply fall to pieces if Jason couldn't attend to them.'

Her tone contained a faint accusation, as though it would be Elinor's fault if Jason didn't make a full recovery.

'You can be quite sure I'll attend to all my responsibilities,' Elinor assured her.

'Well, you'll have Andrew's help soon.'

'Andrew?'

'Jason's GP. Of course he shouldn't really be in general practice at all. He's utterly brilliant. He was offered consultancies by a dozen hospitals, but he's full of ideals.'

She made it sound like an eccentricity. 'He wanted a country practice where he could be useful to people. He's away on holiday, and his deputy is pretty ordinary, I'm afraid. But Andrew will be back in a couple of weeks.'

She sauntered out and a moment later Elinor saw her leap gracefully into the saddle and gallop away. She ground her nails into her palm. She'd known her fair share of insufferable relatives, but something about Lady Virginia Cavenham got under her skin.

'Thank you for not bringing the coffee,' Jason said as soon as she entered. 'Virginia doesn't understand.'

Elinor resisted the temptation to say, she's your fiancée. She ought to understand.

'The next time she's here I'd like to be out of this bed,' Jason said.

'That depends when she'll be coming. If it's tomorrow—'

'Not for a week or two.'

'Then we might have you in a wheelchair by then.' She saw him grip the sheet. 'I'm sorry, Jason, but you're some way off walking.'

'I know that. Actually, I've reached the state where even a wheelchair would be good. You'll have to order it. I've refused to have one in the place until now.'

His next words surprised her. 'I'm not as bad as I seem, Elinor. I'm just not used to being helpless. But I suppose everyone can say that.'

'It's hard for you. I know that.'

'I expect you curse me?'

She drew a swift breath. She had cursed him through long, wretched nights. But not for this.

'Of course not,' she said. 'I can take more than you can throw at me.'

He managed a slight grin. 'You almost tempt me to test that. It might be an interesting challenge.'

'Do so if it amuses you.'

She could have bitten the words back as soon as they were uttered, for Jason's face closed against her again and he said quietly, 'Nothing amuses me these days. Is there any mail left unopened?'

'Just one. It has a London postmark and slightly crabby writing.'

'Probably Carole, my sister-in-law.'

'Your—?'

'She's married to my little brother, Simon. A very nice lady.'

For a moment the world seemed to stop. The paper in her hand wasn't real. The writing wasn't real. The words danced before her in the air. 'Married to my little brother, Simon'.

Simon was married. Simon was married.

I'm going to take you home to meet Jason, and we'll be married as soon as possible.

Now he was married to somebody else. And Jason Tenby had done it to her. All the old bitterness rose up in her, making her choke. She turned away abruptly and went to stand by the window.

'Are you there?' Jason demanded.

'Yes—yes, I'm here.'

'Read me Carole's letter.'

She forced herself to return to the bed and sit down as though nothing had happened.

'"My dear Jason,"' she read, '"I hope, when you receive this, you'll be feeling better than you were when I was at Tenby Manor—"'

'They came up when I had the accident,' Jason broke in, 'and Carole stayed over for a while. Go on.'

'"Simon and I have just got back from the American trip. It was tougher than we'd thought, but we did bring back a few things that will interest you—"'

Jason groaned. 'I knew that trip was a waste of time. We're not geared up to sell to the States. It'll have to come later. But my little brother wanted to take the trip.'

'Just how little is your little brother?' Elinor asked, trying to keep her voice neutral.

'Late twenties.'

'That's not so little. You talk as if he's a boy.'

'He seems like one to me. Too fond of enjoying himself.'

A happy, laughing boy! Until that last day, when he'd turned on her bitterly, because Jason had tricked him into thinking she'd betrayed him.

'"I must admit I really enjoyed New York,"' Elinor read from the letter. '"It became a bit of a second honeymoon. Simon and I are so happy. I couldn't have a more loving husband—"' She stopped because Jason had grunted, but she was glad of the excuse not to read any more. This was harder than she'd feared.

'What's wrong with that?' she said, in answer to his grunt. 'You sound as if you don't believe her.'

'I know she's crazy about Simon and insists on believing the best of him.'

'Maybe a wife should believe the best of her husband,' Elinor suggested quietly.

Jason sighed. 'Well, perhaps it's working out. As I said, she's a nice lady, and Simon said a lot of fine-sounding things about her. According to him she's the love of his life and he'd never known real love until he met her. All that stuff.'

Darling little Cindy, you're the first girl I've ever really

*loved. I never knew it could feel like this. I just know I'll
never love anyone else.*

'All that stuff'…

Jason was talking half to himself. 'Goodness knows, I
did my best to talk him out of it. Maybe I was wrong.'

'You didn't want him to marry her?' Elinor asked
sharply.

'No, I certainly didn't!'

'Wasn't she good enough?'

'I thought she was unsuitable for various reasons—'

'But he wouldn't let you wreck it for him.' Despite her
sadness, Elinor could have cheered for Simon at that moment.

'She's a little older than he is, and— Why am I dis-
cussing this with you? Just read me the rest of the letter.'

Carole praised Simon for another two paragraphs, then
added some more words of comfort before sending her
love and signing off.

When she'd finished Elinor sat in silence; she felt
wrung out. At last she pulled herself together.

'I'll go and see if Hilda's prepared lunch yet.'

'Are you all right?' he asked. 'You sound strange. You
don't mind reading my mail to me, do you?'

'Not at all,' she said firmly.

But she had to stop outside his room, take some deep
breaths and talk to herself severely. Simon had been lost
to her for years, and this was nothing to make a fuss
about. Besides, she didn't really care. She didn't really
care about anything.

When she was quite sure of that she went downstairs.

It took only a short time for Elinor to discover that Jason
created more problems for himself by refusing to

make any adjustment to his changed circumstances. The resulting tension hampered his recovery.

His schedule specified three visits a week from a physiotherapist, but so far these hadn't proved a success. Jason either cancelled appointments or cut them short to take phone calls. Elinor called the therapist, a middle-aged man called Brian with a bad case of ruffled feathers. Under her gentle diplomacy he agreed to try again.

The next step was persuading Jason. He didn't exactly refuse but he made difficulties about dates until she abandoned gentle diplomacy and asked bluntly, 'Do you want to walk again or not?'

'As though being poked around was going to make a difference,' he grumbled.

'Mr Tenby, I don't tell you your business. Please don't tell me mine. The massage is helping to keep your muscles in good order so that they're not wasted by the time you start to regain the feeling. Brian will be here at two o'clock tomorrow afternoon.'

'My factory manager is calling—'

'Then he'll have to wait until Brian has gone.'

Jason drew in his breath sharply. 'You are one stubborn woman.'

'Yes, I am! I'm glad you realise it.'

Brian turned out to be a touchy, nervous little man who irritated Elinor almost as much as he did Jason. He chattered non-stop in a voice that was precisely pitched to drive a blind man crazy. But technically he was excellent at his job. Elinor studied him closely. She knew some physiotherapy, and an idea was forming in her mind.

'I wouldn't want him around me either,' she confessed to Jason when Brian had gone. 'But he knows his stuff.'

She laid out her plan. He would let Brian come once a fortnight if she took over the other sessions, acting on

Brian's instructions. Jason agreed with reluctance, but after the first session he admitted that he felt better.

Elinor knew she had won her first victory, but it was as exhausting as a defeat.

Under her skilful hands Jason became revitalised, but he insisted on staying in touch with the day-to-day running of his empire, and the strain wore out his strength as fast as she revived it. If Elinor ventured to protest she received Jason's snarl.

'You can't go on like this,' she pleaded.

'That's for me to decide.'

'You're not well enough to do *any* work yet, let alone so much.'

'Nurse Smith,' he snapped, 'I have a factory on the verge of expansion, and a twenty-thousand-acre estate to run. Between them they employ fifteen hundred people, who all have bills to pay. They rely on me to provide them with employment and to keep that employment secure so that it will still be there tomorrow. And that can't be done by being ill.'

'But haven't you got managers?'

'Managers!' His voice was scathing. 'Useless. This place works because I keep my finger on the pulse. *My* finger, not somebody else's.'

Elinor had a sudden giddy feeling. This was the old Jason, arrogant, domineering, laying down the law. Even then she might have held her tongue if he hadn't added, 'Now stop arguing about something you know nothing about.'

That was the last straw. Goaded, Elinor did something she'd never done before—lost her temper with a patient. 'I'll tell you one thing I know about,' she declared furiously. 'If your assistants are useless, ask yourself why. Who trained them?'

'What?'

'You're so proud of keeping your finger on the pulse, but if that finger's removed for good you leave everyone else stranded.'

'It isn't going to be removed for good.'

'So you think. But if you go on this way you're headed for a complete collapse. All the people you've encouraged to depend on you will go under, which is about the most selfish thing I've ever heard. And you don't have to throw me out, because I'm going.'

She swept out without waiting for his answer, closing the door sharply behind her.

She was appalled at her own behaviour. She hadn't just given Jason a bracing talk, which would have been justifiable. She'd been overtaken by a personal anger and bitterness which she'd vented on the head of a helpless man.

She could have died of shame.

She fled the house and didn't stop until she was out in the grounds, two hundred yards from the house. She stopped by the lake and hurled a stone far out into its depths, wishing all her problems could be submerged so easily.

What had possessed her to come here? It had always been madness, but at least she'd imagined that she could survive by behaving professionally. Now she knew that after six years this man could still make her act in a way that shamed her.

She'd rushed out without putting on any outdoor clothes, and she shivered as a breeze sprung up.

'I'd better get back and start my packing,' she murmured to herself. 'I'll certainly have to leave here right away.'

Hilda met her on her stairs. 'You're to go straight in,' she said breathlessly. 'Whatever did you do?'

'Told him a few home truths.'

'Oh, dear, oh, dear!'

Taking a deep breath, Elinor pushed open Jason's door and closed it loudly enough to be heard. He turned his head slightly at the sound.

'You shouldn't have stormed off like that.' He sounded tired but calm. 'First rule of straight talking: Stick around to watch the enemy collapse.'

The word 'enemy' took her aback. It was as though he had second sight. 'I apologise for my words,' she said formally. 'I had no right.'

'Second rule: don't spoil it with apologies.'

'That's all very well, but I'm a nurse and what I did was extremely unprofessional.'

'And professionalism is everything to you, isn't it?'

'It matters a great deal,' Elinor said stiffly.

'More than anything else. Why, I wonder?'

Elinor bristled. 'Mr Tenby, I've apologised and I'm willing to leave immediately—'

'Willing to run away, you mean. I thought you were braver than the others.'

'Don't you want me to leave?'

'Come over here.' He held out his hand as though he expected her to take it. She almost did, then drew back and pulled up a chair. After a moment Jason let his hand fall back onto the bed.

'Everything you said was right,' he said. 'I knew it as soon as you spoke. I'd have said so if you'd given me the chance. I hate delegating. But now I know I must let other people do more, just—just until I can take over the reins again.'

Incredibly she realised that he was pleading with her.

He needed to believe that eventually he would recover, because without that hope he couldn't survive. And he was begging her not to deprive him of it.

'Just until then,' she said, and thought she saw him relax.

'You won't go?' he asked.

'No, I won't go.'

'I want your solemn word—I mean, please.'

'You have my solemn word.'

This time there was no doubt. His shoulders sagged as though he'd been holding them tense with anxiety.

'What made you fly out at me like that?' he asked.

'I didn't like seeing all my good work go to waste.'

'Sure there was nothing more?'

Now it was her turn to grow tense. Even with bandages over his eyes Jason saw too much.

'There was nothing more,' she said quickly. 'And I want a promise from you as well. I'll stay on condition that you're a model patient from now on.'

He made a face. 'I don't know how.'

'Don't worry, I'll tell you.'

He gave her a full grin. 'You will too. I'll do my best. Shake on it?'

He offered his hand again and this time she took it.

And for the second time that day she felt herself swept back in time.

On that bright summer day Simon had brought her here and introduced her to his brother, she'd held out her slim hand and it had been swallowed up in Jason's big hard one. He'd held her only lightly, but she could feel the power that radiated from him. It had been like standing in a force field.

She'd adored Simon, but had known instinctively that he was thrown into shadow by his brother.

Now she held Jason's hand again. She could feel how thin he was, how much of his strength was gone, leaving only nervous energy to get him through. And without warning she was swept by a tide of emotion that took her by surprise as surely as the tide of anger had done earlier.

He was so alone as he struggled not to be broken by his ordeal. He wouldn't ask for pity, but he might reach out in a silent plea for friendship. Now his words about her professional standards became a reproach. Clinically she was an excellent nurse, but he needed more, and she'd held it back from him.

A tremor went through her. His hand tightened gently on hers. 'What is it?' he asked.

She tried to control her voice although it still sounded a little husky. 'Nothing. I—I was out in the cold too long. I think I'm getting a sore throat.'

'Then go and get warm quickly. I can't afford you to be ill. You drive me crazy, but I have to admit that you're the only one who knows what she's doing.'

In the days that followed Elinor discovered that their relationship had undergone a mysterious change. It might seem to date from the moment she'd lost her temper and he'd taken it well, but it had more to do with the inch-by-inch developing of respect between them, which had been happening since her arrival.

She couldn't get out of her mind the picture of him holding out his hand to a woman he couldn't see, silently asking for friendship. It would have been too much to say they were actually friends, but they had become comrades in arms, fighting a common enemy.

He didn't stop being difficult, but neither did she stop being stubborn where his welfare was concerned. It became understood between them that strong words could be uttered without resentment on either side. If they disagreed he spoke his mind robustly, but would listen while she did the same. He called her 'the dragon lady', but with a grin that robbed the words of offence.

He smiled more these days and talked with a cheerful air. She wasn't fooled. She knew the demons still raged within his dark prison, but he'd learned to face them down. The horror and dread of the future were still there, but he'd put them to the back of his mind until he knew one way or another.

She wasn't sure what had happened to her hostility.

It hadn't died, but it too seemed to have been put in abeyance until further notice.

'I've brought your mail up,' Elinor said one morning, about ten days after Virginia had left for London. 'There's a pale blue envelope with a London postmark.'

'Virginia. You'd better read that to me.'

'Are you sure you want me to do that?'

'No, but what else do you suggest?'

'Well, Hilda—someone you know well.'

'I think an impersonal voice would work better, don't you?'

He was right, of course. It was just that she was unaccountably reluctant to read Virginia's words of love to him. But there was no choice.

'"My poor dear,"' she read, '"how are you managing without me? Is that dragon of a nurse looking after you properly? Honestly, darling, I don't know where the agency gets them from—"'

'I'm sorry,' Jason broke in. 'You needn't read any more.'

'It's all right, my back is broad,' Elinor replied lightly.

'As you say, it's all impersonal. Where was I? Ah, yes—"don't know where the agency gets them from. Let's hope her nursing skills are better than her social graces."'

'That's because you wouldn't bring me that cup of coffee,' Jason said, grinning.

'You'd said no,' she reminded him.

'And Virginia had said yes. She doesn't like being ignored.'

'But you're my employer, not her.'

'I know. I'm just explaining her point of view so that you understand that she doesn't mean anything by this.'

Elinor could have said that if Virginia truly loved her fiancé she would have tried to sympathise with his point of view. But she maintained a diplomatic silence.

The letter was mostly a recital of Virginia's social round in London, the parties she had been to, the admiration she had received. It was a strange letter to be written to a helpless man, and Elinor wondered just how much of the London whirl Jason saw even when he was well.

'"I can't tell you how much I miss you,"' Elinor read. '"It's so dreadful to think of you lying there, unable to move. But it'll soon be over and we'll be together again—"'

'What is it?' Jason asked, for Elinor had stopped suddenly.

'It's just that—I don't understand. Why can't you be together up here?'

'I beg your pardon?'

'If she misses you so much, why isn't she here?'

'Is that any of your business?' he asked sharply.

'I'm sorry. No, of course it isn't.'

'Give me the letter,' he ordered, reaching out.

Silently she put it into his hand.

'I'm sure you have things to do, Nurse!'

She left the room quietly. Jason listened until the click of the door told him that she'd gone. He was furiously angry.

At thirty-five, Jason Tenby would have proudly boasted that he had never been in love. And if it wasn't entirely true it was true enough to suit him.

He was a red-blooded man, and women had played their part in his life. In his teenage years there had been romps in the hay with local girls whose freely offered charms had briefly beguiled him. And later there had been a satisfying relationship with a widow whose demands on him were few. He'd offered generous help in the support of her two children, and she had always been there when he wanted her. After several years she had married again, and they had parted without pain on either side.

Simon was the opposite of himself. He had a gift for spending money, and a fatal tendency to fall into infatuation. One of these entanglements, in particular, had given Jason nightmares. He'd been uneasy at how drastically he'd been forced to break it, but he'd never doubted that he'd done the right thing.

If it had needed anything to convince him that romantic fancy was more trouble than it was worth, a glance at his brother's colourful life would have done it. He knew that sooner or later he must marry and father the heir that would stop the property falling into Simon's wayward hands.

Virginia was an excellent choice. The daughter of an old family friend, she understood his life, and shared his values if not all of his interests. She enjoyed the social whirl in London, Jason was bored by it. But that was all right. He'd never planned that they should live in each other's pockets. She would make a suitable mistress of

Tenby Manor and mother of Tenby children, and that was all he asked.

Her own view, he guessed, was equally sensible. A man she'd hoped to marry had cried off. She was thirty, and glad to accept a proposal from an old friend. They understood each other.

Elinor's words had galled him because they revealed that she saw him as a man betrayed. He hadn't regarded himself like that, and the suggestion of pity drove him mad.

It wasn't the suspicion that Virginia should have stayed with him, no matter how prosaic their engagement. It was the knowledge, deep within himself, that he'd packed her off to London with a sense of relief.

Elinor seemed to have some romantic idea that a fiancée should be a soul mate. He didn't think of Virginia like that, and he wasn't too sure what a soul mate was.

Possibly someone who understood you so well that they didn't have to ask questions, whose empathy was so deep that they would tolerate your moods without offence; someone whose very presence gave you courage to confront the dark.

As his anger faded he realised that he'd just described Elinor Smith. He grinned, wishing he could tell her. He was sure she would enjoy the joke.

CHAPTER FIVE

ELINOR had managed to persuade Jason to give up sleeping pills for a trial period. To help him sleep she began massaging his neck and shoulders last thing at night, and to her relief it seemed to benefit him. He even admitted as much.

'And it's better than a sleeping pill because it doesn't make me muzzy the next day,' he said one night, pulling off his pyjama jacket and rolling over. 'So I guess you were right.'

'What an admission!' she said cheerfully. 'I know that you'd rather swallow needles than admit I was right about anything.'

'True.'

She began to work on the muscles at the back of his back, which were always in a tight knot by the end of the day. Slowly, under her strong, gentle fingers, they eased.

That night he was in a particularly good mood, having saved an order for his factory.

'The vultures are closing in because they think I'm weak,' he said with a yawn. 'One of them tried to steal my biggest customer. Nearly got away with it, too.'

'How did you manage to stop him?'

'Called the customer, offered him a better deal, sweet-talked him until he didn't know whether he was coming or going.'

'Sweet-talked?' she challenged. 'You?'

'Surprised, huh?'

'Well, I'd imagine the confrontational approach is more your style.'

'Think you know me?'

'I know how much of this area you have under your thumb—'

'I object to the expression ''under your thumb''. It suggests tyranny, and I'm no tyrant. I couldn't run the complex affairs I do if I charged at everything like a bull at a gate.'

'Phooey,' she said provocatively. 'Bull at a gate exactly describes you.'

He lifted his head from the pillow as though trying to hear something in the air. 'Why are you so prejudiced against me?'

'I'm not.'

'You are.'

'You're a powerful man. When all the power is on one side, there's usually someone who comes off worst,' Elinor said at last.

'Who says all the power is on one side? There you go again. When did I turn into a monster?'

When you held me in your arms, against my will, Elinor thought sadly, *and destroyed my heart*.

'You're exaggerating,' she said. 'Or perhaps *I* am. I come from the other side—people without power.'

'And your father's boss was always the enemy, no doubt?'

'My father seldom had a job, but my mother worked.'

'And she had a tyrannical boss?'

Suddenly she saw her first ever meeting with Jason Tenby, long ago, in her childhood, when her mother had taken her to the factory and he'd discovered her.

He'd frowned. 'You shouldn't be here.'

Brenda had appeared quickly. 'We're just leaving, sir.'

'It's Mrs Smith, isn't it?' Even then Jason had known the name and circumstances of every employee. 'I was sorry to hear about your husband's death.' There was a noise behind them. 'Better go quickly now.'

Brenda had seized her daughter's hand and scuttled away, muttering frantically, 'Oh, God, don't let them fire me!'

She hadn't been fired. And next day the foreman had offered her a different shift, at an easier time and at slightly more money.

'Why have you stopped moving?' Jason asked now.

'Sorry.' She began massaging again, working on his broad shoulders.

'Well? What was your mother's boss like?'

'He was generous,' Elinor said slowly. 'In fact, he did her a kindness.'

'But that didn't make you like the poor devil, did it?'

'He did it in such a distant way that it was hard to be grateful.'

'Surely it's the actions that count?'

She could see her mother's tired face glowing as she'd said, 'More money and an easier shift. Oh, love, it'll make all the difference.'

'Yes,' she said. 'It's the actions that count. He meant to be kind. And he was kind.

She wondered why that had never been so clear before.

'If you're the one in charge, you have to be tough,' Jason said.

'But why is it so important to be tough?'

'It's all I know. And if you'd ever met my father you'd understand. He lived and breathed the family tradition, which was that you left the inheritance in better shape than you received it.'

'Suppose you wanted to do something else?' Elinor asked curiously.

'No way. If you were a Tenby you had to be able to run the estates and the factory, and do everything better than your employees.'

'What about—your brother?' she asked, trying to sound natural.

'Simon? Dad wasn't so hard on him. There's eight years between us, and he was spoiled. And he has a lot of charm.' He added wryly, 'He got away with a hell of a lot that I couldn't have.'

'Did you mind that?'

'You mean was I jealous? Is that what you mean?' He sounded outraged.

'It would have been natural if you'd resented the different way you were treated.'

'Well, let me tell you that if you think— Hell, yes! Of course I was jealous. I worked and he slacked. He grew up thinking whatever he wanted was his by right. If there was trouble he charmed his way out of it.'

'You sound as though you don't like him.'

Jason rolled over to confront her, and although she knew that he couldn't see she felt as though he was staring at her.

'Don't like him? He's my brother. He's a Tenby.'

'Does that mean you have to like him?'

'It means I have to stick by him.'

'Tell me about your brother. What was he like?'

It was madness, but she'd lived a sternly disciplined life for too long. Now her parched heart cried out for water in the desert.

'Why do you say *was* like?' Jason demanded. 'He's not dead.'

'Of course not,' she said hastily. 'I only meant—'

She wanted to talk about Simon as he'd been six years ago, her bright, handsome love, with his ready laughter that had lit up the world for her. She wanted Jason to re-create the happiness he'd destroyed. And she'd nearly betrayed herself.

'How can I tell you what he's like? I'm useless with words. Simon's good with them. Too damned good! They've got him into a lot of trouble, and I've always had to pick up the pieces.'

He fell silent again. Elinor's heart was hammering. Was she about to hear her own story?

'You know what I regret?' he said slowly, as if he'd just discovered something.

'Tell me.'

'Not the wrong things I did, or the right things I didn't do. But the things I would have done more cleverly, if I'd known how. You promise yourself that you'll explain later, but suddenly it's too late and you wish—'

He broke off with a little sigh. 'Well, anyway, wishing is no good. I did what I did, and I meant it for the best, but it all went horribly wrong. I just wish I knew how it turned out afterwards.'

'How—what turned out?' she asked slowly.

He yawned. Her work was having its effect.

'We never really know—do we?—what we're doing to other people. I thought it would be all right, but she cried—I've never heard anyone cry like that.'

She took his hand. 'Jason—'

'Don't go away,' he said quietly.

She said nothing, but sat there with his hand in hers. His grip tightened, then relaxed again. He slept.

Elinor sat by the bed, not moving, her hand still in his, pondering his words. They might have meant anything. Why should she think he was talking about the girl whose heart he'd broken long ago? Yet the thought wouldn't leave her.

'You're right,' she whispered to him. 'We never know what we're doing to other people. And perhaps it's better that we don't. What can we do about it when it's too late?'

Obeying an impulse she didn't understand, she raised his hand and brushed it against her cheek. Then she hurried from the room.

After she'd let him into Jason's room, Elinor's relationship with Bob improved. When she took her daily walk he would come with her, and they were soon fast friends.

Now the rain had stopped and the sun grew stronger, the land was richer with daffodils and buttercups. Blackthorn shone in the hedges, primroses glowed in the woods, marsh marigold bloomed by the stream.

In the middle of April Elinor strode out, wearing jeans and baggy sweater, her hair swinging free. Bob bounded up, a ball in his mouth.

'All right,' she laughed, touched by his hopeful expression. 'Let's have a game.'

She threw the ball and he went racing away after it, ears flying. She ran after him, scooped up the ball and threw it again. For a few moments she could leave her cares behind and enjoy herself in the company of a creature to whom everything was simple.

Bob raced back to drop the ball at her feet. She seized it up, but instead of throwing it she held it out of reach, laughing and teasing him, while he barked madly. At last he managed an impossibly high leap, caught his teeth in the arm of her sweater and pulled her off balance. Her feet slipped away, and the next moment they were rolling together down a steep incline, heading for the lane that led from the road to the house.

At the very last moment Elinor was aware of a car braking sharply and the long, protesting sound of a horn. She was sprawling in the dusty road, practically under the car's wheels.

'Have you got a death wish?' demanded an indignant male voice.

She hastily scrambled to her feet, realising what a sight she looked. The incline had been covered with wild flowers, and now she was covered with them too. She pulled some primroses out of her hair.

'I'm sorry,' she said self-consciously. 'It was an accident.'

The driver was a stocky man in his mid-thirties, with a broad, dependable face.

'Of all the daft, lame-brained—' He stopped with a sigh. 'You've cut your hand. I'm a doctor. When we get to the house I'll have a look at you.'

'Thank you, but apart from that scratch I'm not hurt.'

'That's for me to say.'

'I'm a nurse and I assure you I'm not hurt.'

'A nurse? Good grief! Don't tell me they've actually entrusted you with that sick man in there? Heaven help him!'

'I'm Nurse Elinor Smith,' she said indignantly. 'And fully qualified.'

'What in? Idiocy? Fooling around with dogs?'

'I'm off duty, for pity's sake!'

He grinned. Nature seemed to have designed his homely face for good humour. 'I'm Dr Andrew Harper. I heard that yet another new nurse had arrived. I know what Jason can be like, but it's a bit soon for you to be hurling yourself under a car, isn't it? Get in, instead.'

She did so, regarding him askance. Bob jumped in after her. As they drove back to the house she studied him.

Andrew Harper was heavily built with light brown, receding hair and bushy eyebrows. He wore a tweed jacket that had obviously once been expensive but had now reached the comfortably shabby stage.

'I've really been looking forward to meeting you,' she said lightly.

'I'm suspicious about the way you said that. I sense a trap being laid for me.'

'The Lady Virginia told me to expect a paragon of medical genius.'

He groaned. 'Oh, heavens! What's she been saying now? No, let me guess. I'm far too skilled for mere country practice. All the very best hospitals were competing for my services. Is that right?'

'Not quite,' she said with a smile. 'She only said "hospitals". You added that they were the very best.'

He winced. 'I walked right into that, didn't I?'

'Isn't it all true?'

'Virginia's my cousin. She rather feels that I've blotted her family name by choosing country practice.'

'You mean you're a member of the "upper crust" too?' she teased.

'Fraid so. The difference between Virginia and me is that it defines her world, and I couldn't care less.'

'Then you must know Jason pretty well.'

'We were at school together, fought over the same girls, defended each other to the death against outsiders. Poor fellow.'

'He's allowed me to order a wheelchair. I'm expecting it any day.'

'Good. Getting out of that room might brighten him up.'

On arrival at the house, they mounted the stairs together. As they reached Jason's room Andrew stopped and reached out to pluck something from her hair. 'You missed one,' he said, showing her a yellow primrose.

She laughed. 'I'd better change out of these dirty clothes.'

Andrew's eyebrows went up when he saw her turn into her tiny bedroom. He gave her a considering look, but said nothing as he went in to see Jason.

The two men greeted each other with the ease of long friendship. Jason met Andrew's enquiry with a violent curse that made him feel slightly better.

'I know,' Andrew said sympathetically. 'It's damnable.'

'When does it end? When do I get up? When do I see? And don't tell me to be patient or I'll chuck something at you.'

'I wouldn't tell you a damn fool thing like that. I know it's hard, Jason, but healing has to happen in its own good time.'

'You sound like Nurse Smith. Have you met her?'

'I'll say I have. Just now. I nearly ran her over. She just appeared out of the earth like a wood nymph.'

'Like a what? Is that you being poetic, Andrew?'

The doctor gave a self-conscious laugh. 'Guess it is. Meeting a miracle tends to bring out the poet in a man. How can such a divine creature be called something as ordinary as Smith?'

'Divine creature?' Jason echoed, puzzled. 'She's a dragon: a nice dragon, but she still breathes fire. Her first day here, I asked what she looked like, and she told me she wore a white uniform, black stockings and sensible shoes.'

Andrew laughed. 'When I saw her she was wearing

jeans and sweater, sprawling in the dust like an urchin, with her hair falling over her eyes.'

'What colour is her hair? It's no use my asking her.'

'So she's preserving a professional distance. Very proper.'

Suddenly Jason was back in the strangest dream he'd ever had. He could see again, but he couldn't make out the face of the woman in his arms. He could feel her, smell the scent of wild flowers, hear her softly murmuring voice. But her face was hidden, until she turned to him suddenly and he saw that she was someone he flinched from remembering. He tried to protest but her lips were soft and inviting against his.

He shook his head to clear it. Why should that dream have come to torment him now? And why did he keep getting flashbacks in the day?

'What did you say?' he asked Andrew vaguely.

'I said your nurse is preserving a professional distance.'

'Yes,' he said, dazed. 'Of course she is.' He pulled himself together. 'Describe her.'

'She's young, in her twenties, and she's got fair hair, falling around her shoulders and full of flowers. She was picking them out as we talked.'

'Wild flowers in her hair,' Jason murmured. 'Yes, that's how I—' He checked himself and coloured. 'Is she tall or short?' he demanded.

'Divinely tall, like the stem of a flower, with the longest legs. Her eyes are as blue as the lake in summer…'

He rambled on, using terms that might have been excessive for a pagan goddess. Jason listened with interest, trying to reconcile this vision of perfection with the stern Nurse Smith.

'How did she come to have flowers in her hair?' he asked.

'She was playing with Bob. He tripped her and she fell down the bank right under my wheels. I only just stopped in time.'

'At which, naturally, you fell instantly in love with her,' Jason said caustically.

'Don't jest, you sacrilegious man. She's an invitation to love, with a smile like the sun.'

'Elinor? Are you off your head?'

'I've been off my head for the last hour.'

Jason heard the door click, then Elinor's cool, correct voice. 'Good afternoon, Doctor.'

'Good afternoon, Nurse,' Dr Harper returned.

'What's she wearing now, Andrew?' Jason demanded.

'A uniform,' he replied. 'White, starchy and very proper.'

'I told you never to wear that thing,' Jason said, revolted.

'I'm wearing it now out of respect for the doctor.'

'Let me see your hand,' Andrew insisted.

'I've taken care of it.' Elinor showed him the sticking plaster she'd put over the wound. 'Hey, what are you doing?'

'Giving you a proper dressing, as I told you I was going to,' he said firmly.

'Are you suggesting I'm incapable of doing a simple dressing?'

'I'm sure you managed as well as you could with one hand, but I'm using two hands, so I'll make a better job. Now keep still and stop arguing.'

Jason gave a sigh of pure pleasure. 'You don't know how much I'm enjoying hearing the bossy Nurse Smith on the receiving end.'

But his cheerful mood was brief. A moment later Elinor gave a chuckle and he stiffened. What had happened to cause her to laugh? How did it make her look? Did her eyes glow as delightfully as her voice suggested?

And what a change in sound. Usually her voice was so controlled that he found it impossible to picture the woman. But for a fleeting moment it had a richness that hinted at another side to her—no, ten other sides, all of them inviting a man to venture further. It dawned on him for the first time that Elinor was not only a nurse but a woman.

There was a knock on the door and Hilda's voice said, 'It's here. They've just delivered the chair downstairs.'

'I'll come down,' Elinor said.

'Andrew,' Jason said urgently as soon as she'd gone, 'if it is that wheelchair, I want you to help me into it. Send the women away, even Elinor.'

'You're going to have to let her help you with it eventually.'

'I know. But give me a chance to get the hang of it first. You know what I'm like. I can't stand anyone seeing me helpless. And especially her.'

'What's wrong with her?'

'Nothing. She's the best nurse I've had. But there's something elusive about her.'

He knew he was putting it badly. Words came hard to him, or he might have said that as well as being elusive Elinor was also restful, because he always knew where he was with her. And if that was a contradiction of 'elusive', well, that was just another thing he couldn't find the words to explain. He only knew that both were true.

The chair was brought to Jason's room, and set up. Elinor caught the look in Andrew's eye, nodded her understanding, and left the room.

A few minutes later Andrew appeared pushing the wheelchair, which he brought slowly down the stairs.

Something strange happened to Elinor as she saw the sightless figure, his hands lying uselessly on his lap. A pang of some unfamiliar emotion swept over her, giving her a sense of danger. She didn't examine it too closely. It was alarmingly like pity.

Pity for her patients was something Elinor kept under control. It damaged her judgement. But suddenly her control slipped, and she was swept by such a feeling of despair that it seemed that she was linked directly with the heart of the stricken man.

To live out a useless life, to be helpless and undignified when you'd been used to power and action—could any horror compare to it?

The moment passed. But she was left shaken, no longer quite the same person she had been before.

They wheeled Jason outside, and he lifted his head to inhale the fresh air, taking deep, luxurious breaths.

'It's good to be out,' he said at last. 'Let's have some tea out here.'

'I'll fetch it,' Elinor said quickly. She needed to get away from Jason until she'd sorted out her thoughts. He would be all right in Andrew's company.

But while she was preparing the tray in the kitchen Andrew hurried in, his mobile phone still in his hand.

'I've got to go,' he said. 'Emergency. But I'll be back soon, and I'd like us to meet up some time for a long talk.'

'Yes, that would be a good idea.'

She took the tray out to the stone terrace where Jason was sitting and explained Andrew's departure.

Jason no longer wore bandages about his eyes, but a black mask. The wounds had healed, but his eyes must be shielded from light for some time longer. To remove the mask too soon would be to invite disaster. Now he raised his face to the sun, smiling a little as he felt it warm his skin.

'It's a lovely day,' he said. 'I can feel it. Soon perhaps—' He broke off and said quickly, 'Don't say anything. I've no right to ask you to build up my hopes.'

'Of course you have. Who should you ask if not me?'

'I promised myself not to give way to self-pity.'

'No, self-pity wouldn't be like you,' she said, meaning it.

'I'm not so sure. Haven't I been sorry for myself? Railing against the world. Attacking anyone who tries to help me. I could at least try to act civilised, couldn't I?'

His insight touched her. While she tried to frame an answer he said, 'It's all right. You can give it to me straight.'

'I don't need to,' she said gently. 'You've seen it for yourself. You've done what no nurse could do for you.'

'No other nurse. But you—' He stretched out his hand and after a moment she took it. 'You're different. Be a little patient with me. I'm getting there.'

She squeezed his hand and felt him squeeze back.

'Friends?' he asked.

'Friends.'

There was no other reply she could make. 'Friends' wasn't quite true. But what was true? She was no longer sure.

CHAPTER SIX

ELINOR was awoken by a scream that seemed to come from hell. She was alert in an instant, leaping out of bed and tearing across the hall to Jason's room. He was thrashing about on the bed, desperately fighting something, trying to shield his face with his arms.

'No!' he screamed. *'No, no!'*

'Jason, wake up,' she cried, trying to pierce the madness of his terror. 'Wake up! It's all right. It's only a dream. For God's sake, wake up!'

He couldn't hear her. Whatever horror had him in his grip it was refusing to release him. His blindness made it worse. A sighted man could have opened his eyes and the reality of his surroundings would have driven the dream away. But no such escape was possible for Jason. He stayed trapped in his nightmare, thrashing and struggling until she was seriously alarmed in case he did further damage to his injured back.

She put her arms firmly about him, holding him as still as she could. 'Jason, wake up! Please wake up! It's all right. It's over. I'm here.'

At last her voice seemed to get through to him. He stopped struggling and lay in her arms, trembling, exhausted.

'Oh, God!' he whispered. 'Oh, God!'

He clung to her, oblivious to all else but his despair. In his blind need for comfort he reached out to her, wrapping his arms about her, burying his face in her warm flesh.

Elinor responded instinctively, enfolding him in her

arms, drawing him closer. At this moment she was all
nurse, desperate to do what would ease her tormented patient. His head fit naturally against her breasts, and the
words she spoke seemed to come of their own accord.

'It's all right. I'm here. Jason—Jason—'

'Hold onto me,' he choked. 'I can't bear it—'

'My dear—' She hardly knew she'd said it, but she had
a sudden disconcerting sensation at the feel of him pressed
close against her. It was nothing to do with the sedate
pleasure she normally felt while comforting a patient. It
was wild, turbulent and shockingly sweet. She wanted to
hold his head against her for ever, whispering soft, intimate words of consolation.

'What do you dream?' she asked. 'Can you tell me?'

'It's the fire. I'm back in it—fighting to find a way
through—but I'm lost—I can't see my way out—and the
heat is terrible.' He gave a long shudder. 'In my dream I
can see again—flames—then it all falls in on me, and
everything goes dark. But I can still feel the heat—and—
and the terror—'

It cost him a lot to admit his fear, but he was sinking
into a black pit, frantically reaching for hands to save him.

'How often do you have this dream?'

'It's been a while since last time. I thought I was safe,
but tonight it came back.'

'You've been working too hard and you've had a reaction. Are you fully awake now?'

'Yes, I'm awake,' he said wearily. 'If you can call it
being awake. The nightmare's always there, waking or
sleeping. In the end, there's no escape. There never will
be.'

She wanted to tell him that his sight would return and
he would see a way out of the horror. But she wasn't
completely sure, and she couldn't offer less than honesty

to this tortured man. He felt her hesitation, and his grip
on her tightened.

'It's true, isn't it?' he said harshly. 'I'm blind for good.'

'I don't know,' she whispered.

'Help me, Elinor! *Help me, for God's sake!*'

In his desperation he reached up for the mask over his
eyes. His fingers curled over the edges. She moved
quickly to stop him.

'No! Jason, no!'

'I've got to find out!' he shouted. 'Do you think I can
stand not knowing?'

'But it's too soon,' she pleaded. 'Jason, you can only
do harm like this. Don't throw your chance away.'

'There's no chance, and you know it. Let's have the
truth at once.'

'No!' Putting out all her strength, Elinor forced him to
relinquish his hold. He gave up the fight and collapsed
into her arms. She could feel the strength drain out of
him.

She abandoned words, for words could be of no use to
him. Only her tenderness might help, and that she offered
him in abundance.

She'd dashed from her bed too fast to put on a dressing
gown and now she remembered that she was wearing only
a thin nightdress with narrow straps that left her shoulders
and arms bare. She had the alarming realisation that she
was almost naked. She would have covered herself, but
she had nothing to do it with.

Gradually she forgot about everything else but the sensation of his face against her, and the warmth from his
body intermingling with her own and spreading out to
engulf her until she was all heat from her crown to her
toes.

She gasped and tried to free herself. At least, she

thought she did—she was sure she did—but when she looked at her hands they were still cradling him, and if they moved at all it was only to hold him more firmly. She meant to push him away, but her limbs refused to do her bidding. They had a will of their own, and they wanted to hold him.

Jason's body was shaken by tremors as though all the horror he'd been repressing had caught up with him suddenly and would no longer be denied. He held her like a man clinging to a life raft.

'It's all right, I'm here,' she murmured. She'd said the words a thousand times before, but they'd never had such meaning until now.

'Thank God,' he groaned. 'If you weren't here I don't think I could cope. I thought I was strong, but there's nothing left. Just the pit, waiting for me—don't let me go.'

She tightened her arms and dropped her head so that her lips brushed his forehead. 'No,' she murmured. 'Feel me holding you.'

Gradually his breathing grew slower and more controlled, but she knew his nightmare wasn't over. It had merely moved into another stage.

'Talk to me, Jason,' she said. 'Tell me everything about that night.'

'Dear God,' he murmured, 'haven't I lived through it enough already?'

'Yes, but we have to deal with it so that it goes away. Trust me.'

She saw his forehead crease into a frown. With one hand he reached up. He found her face, the hair hanging down her neck to her breasts.

'You really are there?' he whispered. 'You seem no

more than a dream—a voice in the darkness; one day I'll call and you won't be there.'

'I'm here, I'm here,' she said urgently. 'Feel me. I'm real.'

'Sometimes you're the only real thing in the world.'

'Talk to me. Trust me. What happened that night?'

'I was working late. I stepped out for a breath of fresh air and saw the smoke. I raised the alarm, and ran to the stables—' He stopped.

'And then?'

He flinched back. 'I don't want to go in there,' he said hoarsely.

He could see it—the flames, the brilliant red glow within the stable, the flickering straw: the last things his eyes had ever seen, the images burned onto them forever.

'You must,' she said gently. 'You can't change it, but you can turn it into something you can cope with. Go on.'

He took a breath. 'It wasn't too bad at first. I went for the horses near the door—got them out quickly. There was a stable hand working with me—he took one side, I took the other—'

'Did you get the horses out fairly easily?'

'At first—they were kicking and it was hard to get near them, but we opened the doors and they bolted out—they could see the outside world so they knew where they were going.' He stopped. He was trembling.

'It was so hot in there,' he went on after a moment. 'I could hear the flames and hear the horses screaming with fear. We'd got most of them out—but I could hear them calling from the far end. The sweat was pouring off me—into my eyes—' He stopped.

'What is it?' Elinor asked.

'I didn't want to go back in—I'd have given anything not to—but the others were going in—young lads; I couldn't let them do it alone—and I thought I could hear Damon. He's my own horse. I could hear him but I couldn't see him for smoke—I was sure he was there...

'But he wasn't. I hunted around in the smoke—I thought my lungs would burst—then I heard something overhead and looked up— *Are you there?*'

'Yes, I'm here, I'm here,' she said urgently. 'Take my hand. There, hold me.'

He gripped her so tightly that the pressure was agonising, but she didn't try to pull away.

'And then?' she asked.

'No—no more! You're like those damned psychiatrists who tried to get me to talk in the hospital.'

'No, I'm not like them. I'm your friend, Jason. I won't leave after an hour. I'll be here as long as you want me. And the next time your mind is trapped in that stable I'll still be there. Try to tell me what happened next.'

He shuddered, and she could feel the effort it cost him, but after a moment he went on.

'I look up—and the fire is so brilliant that I can see it through the smoke. And then the beam comes down towards me through the flames. That's the last thing I see— but I can still hear—the screams—the roaring of the flames— *Where are you?*'

'Here. Here.' She enfolded him. 'Don't listen to the flames. Listen to me. I'm here, Jason, I'm here.'

'If only you'd been there then,' he murmured. 'Nothing could have happened to me.'

'What happened to the others? The stable hands, the horses.'

'They all got out.'

'Was anyone else hurt?'

'They tell me not. I've talked to the hands and they say they're fine, and all the horses were got out in time.'

'But you don't really believe that, do you?'

'Of course I—if they tell me—they're all safe.'

'Yes, of course they're safe,' she agreed. 'The only one hurt was you.'

She was still holding him. Gradually she felt his trembling slow until it stopped altogether. She laid him back on the pillow, but kept hold of his hand. The violence of his nightmare was taking its toll and his exhaustion was clear, but he seemed more at peace.

'I'm glad you were so close,' he murmured. 'Across the corridor—'

'Go to sleep,' she whispered. 'I wouldn't go when you tried to throw me out. I won't go now you want me.'

He smiled faintly. 'Stubborn.'

'As a mule,' she confirmed. 'Like you.'

'Mmm!'

When she was sure Jason was asleep Elinor quietly left him and returned to her own room. She didn't go straight to bed, but went to the window and drew back the curtain a few inches.

It was five o'clock, and the first grey hint of dawn was already softening the darkness. The trees rustled in the breeze, and all around her was the beauty of a spring morning.

But Elinor barely noticed. She was gazing into the distance, trying to come to terms with the fact that tonight she had held her enemy in her arms, and it had been the sweetest experience of her life.

They breakfasted together in the conservatory. The suffering of the night was still on his face, but he was calm and collected. Elinor wondered how it would be if he could see. Would he be able to meet her eyes? Or was he ashamed now that she'd witnessed his weakness?

'Is the weather good enough to go out?' he asked.

'Yes, it's a lovely day.'

'Then take me out under the trees, and we'll talk.'

There was something in his quiet voice that she'd never heard before.

They wandered for a while, enjoying the lovely day. Jason threw the ball for Bob, who tore after it and dropped it back at his feet, for Elinor to retrieve and put into his hands. He made no protest at being helped like this, and she began to feel that she knew what he wanted to talk about.

At last, when she was sitting on a log near him, he said, 'I guess I can accept it now. I'm not giving in, Elinor, but raging doesn't help, does it?'

'No, it doesn't help,' she agreed.

'But where do I go from here? What's the next step?'

'You might still get your sight and movement back,' she began carefully.

'But I guess the odds are against that—at least for both of them.'

'Jason, I don't have a crystal ball—'

'No, it's all right. I've been trying to face the worst. I tell myself I couldn't stand it, but if I had to I'd give it my best shot—if only I knew the right place to start.'

'There's no right place,' she murmured.

'What?'

'The right place is everywhere and all the time. You can't look for it. It's just there, moment by moment.'

He turned his head to her with an oddly alert movement. 'You know, don't you?'

Suddenly she saw the danger and backed off. 'Everybody knows—in their own way.'

'No, you know. Something happened to you. You understand things that other people don't. I've always sensed that. Can't you tell me?'

'It's nothing, Jason,' she said quickly. 'You've got it all wrong; you're imagining everything. Here, boy, fetch!'

She sprang up and hurled the ball for Bob, who chased it, barking madly. She was shaking at what had so nearly happened. For a moment everything had vanished except Jason and his needs, and in her yearning to help him she'd taken the first steps onto treacherous ground. But she'd seen the danger in time, she told herself frantically. She could still retreat back into the numb place deep within herself where all pain was smothered; the place where she was safe, because if you didn't feel you couldn't be hurt.

She turned back, ready to face Jason's annoyance at the way she'd abruptly abandoned him. But there was no anger. He sat with his head slightly on one side, as if he was puzzled. She felt a pang of remorse. He'd asked for her help and she'd refused. If he would only shout and condemn her she would feel better. But he looked too battered to fight, and she couldn't bear it.

She rehearsed the words 'I'll tell you anything you need if only it will help you'.

But what came out was, 'There's a breeze coming up. I think we should be getting back.'

'Yes, of course,' he said politely.

She wheeled him towards the house, but at the last moment she paused. 'I know the stables have been rebuilt in the last few weeks. Perhaps you should visit them.'

'Are you sure that's a good idea?' he said reluctantly.

'I think you'll be glad you did.'

She headed around the left wing of the house and across the yard. Already they could both hear the sounds of horses snorting and hooves on the cobblestones.

A chestnut mare was being led out by a stable hand, a

middle-aged man with a weather-beaten face. When he saw his employer he grinned and yelled, 'Hey!'

'Fred!' Jason pronounced, and the next moment his hand was seized.

'It's good to see you back,' he said.

The horse gave a noisy snort, and Jason reached up to touch its nose with a smile of pleasure.

'Dandy's glad to see you and all,' Fred declared, almost dancing with delight.

Elinor watched as Jason gently brushed Dandy's nose, and felt the hot breath against his hands.

'There, boy,' he said softly, and turned his head so that his cheek rested against the velvet nose. It was hard to tell what was happening to his eyes behind the mask, but Elinor saw his brows contract as though with some emotion.

'What's the new building like, Fred?' Jason asked after a while.

'It's grand,' Fred asserted. 'I made improvements like you said, and it's like a palace for them now. Shall I take you around?'

'No, you give Dandy his gallop,' Jason said quickly. 'I'll just wander around.'

When they were alone he said to Elinor, 'All right. You can take me in now.'

The new stable building was large and airy, with a skylight to let in natural light. Five stalls lined each wall, and long noses looked over curiously as they made their way along.

Elinor stopped by every stall, allowing Jason time to touch the animal and feel for himself that it was unhurt. At first she read out the names that were written up, but soon he stopped her.

'Don't tell me, let me guess. They're all individuals. This one's Tansy, right?'

'Right.'

'She's a young mare; I've had her about three years. She turned out a bit slower than I'd hoped but she's so affectionate I can't bear to get rid of her.'

Tansy was nibbling him as he spoke, and he laughed softly, turning his head to avoid her over-eager caresses. His affection for the horses transformed him.

At the next stall it was the same story. 'Hey, come on, Rosie,' he laughed, fending her off and kissing her at the same time. 'It is Rosie, isn't it?'

'Yes,' Elinor said lightly. Rosie was the horse who'd once dumped her in the stream.

'She's a tease, this one,' Jason said. 'She's gentle enough, but full of tricks. You never knew where you'd end up. She dumped one rider in the water. Mind you, it was the silly girl's own fault, pretending to ride when she couldn't.'

'How foolish of her,' Elinor said coolly. 'Shall we go on to the next?'

The animal in the next stall was already snorting and pawing the ground as he recognised Jason.

'Damon!' his master greeted him. 'Let me feel you. You're really all right?'

He ran his hands over as much as he could reach of the animal's black, satiny skin, and seemed to be satisfied.

'Yes,' he murmured. 'Yes.'

They spent a little longer in the stables, going around slowly so that Jason could feel everything.

'I'd like to go back now,' he said at last.

She took him into the house, where his secretary was waiting.

'Are you all right, Jason?' she asked.

'Yes, I'm fine. Thank you, Elinor. I guess I know why you did that. It's real now. The horses are real, and everything. Just being told they were unhurt wasn't the same, but now I've felt them for myself. And also—'

'Yes?'

'I don't know—never mind. It's all right.'

He didn't know how to say what was in his mind—that the next time his nightmares led him into the burning stables he wouldn't be alone. She would be there. And it would be less terrible.

After that they visited the stables every day. The hands would greet him with pleasure, and the mere proximity to the horses seemed to do Jason good.

The weather was rapidly growing warmer, and each afternoon Elinor would insist on a trip out in the fresh air. He talked more cheerfully now, although she knew he often had to force himself. Jason Tenby had been reared to do the right thing, and he'd decided that the right thing was to appear cheerful, no matter what the cost.

When the strain of putting on a bright face became too much for him he would growl at Elinor, but in a resigned, half-humorous way that she would return with interest.

She watched his lonely struggle, helping when she could, but knowing that his salvation could be found only in himself.

One afternoon, when his secretary had just left, she found Jason in the study, drumming his fingers on his desk.

'It's not her fault,' he said tensely, when he knew it was Elinor. 'It's not her fault. I know it isn't. I keep telling myself it isn't.'

'Her? Who?'

'Miss Horton. She's a good secretary, but she's got a

voice like something squeaking on glass. I never noticed it before, but ten minutes of listening to her reading aloud and I'm ready to bang my head against the wall. Why can't everyone have a voice like yours?'

'I'll read your business mail as well as the personal stuff if you like. You could dictate the replies into a machine.'

'I've got a machine. I can't find half the damned knobs.'

'Then we'll get you another one with easier-to-find knobs,' she said soothingly.

'You're managing me, you terrible woman!'

'Just trying to make your life easier.'

'Grrr!'

'Jason—'

'All right, all right, I'm intolerable. Let's take that as read.'

'Sure we will. I'm shaking in my shoes.'

'It would be nice to make you shake in your shoes,' he grumbled. 'You insufferable, superior, know-everything *nurse*!'

'Is "nurse" the worst thing you can call me?' she challenged.

'If I knew of something worse I'd use it.'

His manner was droll rather than hostile, and she laughed aloud. After a moment he gave a reluctant grin.

'Oh, the hell with it! Rescue me, Elinor. I'm going crazy.'

The upshot was that she drove into Hampton Tenby and found him a machine that he could use with ease. After that she read all the estate mail to him, he dictated his answers into the machine, and Miss Horton prepared the letters next day.

Elinor had also exercised her diplomatic skills on Hilda

to persuade her to lighten Jason's diet. Some of the heavier meals disappeared, replaced by omelettes and fruit. The patient stopped leaving his food and began to fill out satisfactorily.

'I don't know how I ever managed without you,' he said one night when she was putting him to bed. 'I suppose all your patients say that?'

'I've never had another patient like you.'

'You forgot to add "Thank goodness".'

'Maybe I did,' she said, laughing. 'Now, goodnight.'

CHAPTER SEVEN

ALMOST the worst job Elinor had to do was testing Jason's reflexes and finding, every day, that there was no more life in his legs than there had been the day before. If he were ever to walk again he should be regaining some feeling now, and they both knew it.

Her skilful work massaging and flexing his legs had ensured that the muscles had regained much of their strength, and when needed they were ready for action. But their healthy look only made a mockery of their uselessness.

When each day's disappointment came he shrugged and immediately began to discuss something else. Only a kind of suppressed pain in his manner betrayed the withering of hope, and when she next saw him even that would have gone, replaced by an air of cheerfulness that didn't fool her.

If she had wanted revenge, she was having it now, in full. Instead, she felt only a growing ache in her heart, and a raging helplessness that she could do nothing for him.

Once, without meaning to, she revealed her frustration. 'Don't get upset,' he said kindly. 'You make it bearable. God knows, it's bad enough, but without you it would have been a thousand times worse.'

Now, to her growing sadness for him was added a sense of guilt at the deception she'd practised so innocently. She could bear anything except his kindness.

She would scour the radio magazines to find plays and

discussions that would interest him, and in the evenings they would listen together. He could listen to a play alone but not a talk, because the opinions usually infuriated him so much that he needed someone to rage at. Elinor would oppose him just enough to be provocative and they would have lively arguments that prevented his spirits sinking too far.

They found a shared interest. Both enjoyed detective stories and television police shows. In Elinor's company he would even listen to the television, relying on her to explain the action. His managers still visited him for instructions and gradually he got a hold of the business that had slipped away from him in the hospital. It was life of a kind. And for a man with no eyes or legs it was a remarkably full life. But she knew he was slowly going mad.

She'd trained herself to sleep lightly, half alert for her patient. Now she found it hard to sleep at all, constantly listening for any sound that indicated Jason was suffering. If he seemed restless she would drop in, apparently casually, offer him a cup of hot milk, and end up taking him a whisky and soda, with ice, just as he liked it.

'There isn't one woman in a thousand can pour a perfect whisky,' he said one night, 'but you got it right first time. Exactly two fingers and a brief dash of soda, just as I like it. Are you clairvoyant or something?'

That had been one of her slips—pouring his whisky without asking how he liked it, because she remembered from the past. But she glided out of it neatly.

'Of course I'm clairvoyant. And I shouldn't be pouring one for you at this hour either, but if I didn't you'd only shout and frighten me.'

He gave a snort of amusement. 'Frighten the dragon lady?'

'A moment ago I was a woman in a thousand,' she joked.

'You are. You're also intolerable.'

She laughed, not at all offended. 'You only say that because I'm the first nurse you haven't been able to bully.'

'It's a slander. I'm the mildest of men.'

'Of course you are, as long as the world is dancing to your tune.'

'Well,' he said with a sigh, 'it's not dancing to my tune now, is it?'

'I'm sorry, Jason—'

'It's all right. One little remark isn't going to floor me. I'm tough. Pour me another whisky and go back to bed. The way I treat you, you need all the sleep you can get.'

Jason liked to mull over the problems of the estate and the factory with Elinor while she was working on his legs. She said little beyond 'Yes', 'No', and 'How did you deal with that?' But this was all he wanted. It gave him the chance to sort his thoughts out.

'I just wish I could get back to the factory,' he groaned one day.

'I can drive you over one day.'

'A blind man in a wheelchair? No way. When I go back I go on my feet.'

'We'll work for that,' she assured him.

He talked on for a while. Elinor had been awake most of the night, so although it was morning she was tired, and answered mechanically. She thought he didn't notice, but at last he stopped and said, 'Is something wrong?'

'No, nothing.'

'I wonder? If there was something troubling you, that strict professionalism of yours wouldn't let you tell me, would it?'

'Of course not. I'm here to take care of your troubles, not my own.'

'Don't you think I spend enough time brooding about my own troubles? Thinking about yours might do me good.'

'But I don't have any troubles,' she said firmly.

After a moment Jason said, 'You're a liar, Nurse Smith. Your voice is full of trouble.'

'Jason, please—'

'Dammit, can't you stop being a nurse for five minutes? You know what could happen if I was a normal man?'

'You *are*—'

'I could ask you to have dinner with me—nothing heavy, just a pleasant evening, talking over a meal and a glass of wine. We'd talk about me, but also about you. You'd tell me about yourself, about your hopes and dreams, and the life that's made you the person you are. But because I'm a blind cripple you know everything about me, and I know nothing about you. Can you imagine how humiliating that is?'

'That's not fair, Jason. You make it sound as though it's all my fault, but it's just the way it is between a nurse and her patient—'

'But I don't want to be a patient. I want to be a man.'

'I'm sorry,' she said distractedly. 'I should have understood how you must feel and—'

'Stop damned well apologising!' he said in agony. 'Stop humouring me, patronising me.'

'I—' She stopped on the verge of the fatal words.

'If you say you're sorry, I'll chuck something,' he threatened.

Silence.

'Interesting, isn't it?' he jeered. 'When you can't talk like a nurse you can't talk at all.'

'Well, what do you want me to say?' she demanded, goaded. 'That your temper's atrocious?'

'It would be the truth.'

'Then why would you expect me to want to have dinner with you?' she retorted. 'You want to be treated like a normal man—act like one. Stop bawling me out when I say a word out of place, and if you can talk to me nicely for five minutes on end maybe—maybe I'll say yes.'

'Well, that's honest,' he said after a moment.

'Yes, it is,' she said crossly. She was feeling too weary to be diplomatic. 'And honest is what you asked for.'

'That's right. I asked for it, and I got it. Oh, boy, did I get it! I'm not sure that I'm going to ask you to dinner, Dragon Lady.'

'Fine! Don't!'

'Well, you wouldn't have come anyway. My dining room is great on history but not strong on entertaining a lady. Plenty of ancestors on the walls, but where's the atmosphere, the soft lights, the music, the top class food and wine?'

'Food doesn't come any more top class than Hilda's and she tells me you have an excellent cellar.'

'So you accept?'

'Yes!'

Like someone who saw the step too late to avoid tripping, she'd spotted the danger and walked into it all in one split second. She regarded him with exasperation.

'You tricked me!'

'Sure I did. It feels wonderful to have out-thought the Dragon Lady.'

'Will you stop calling me that?'

'Nope!' His expression was triumphant.

Exasperation changed to resignation, and from there it

was only a short step to tenderness. He had so little. How could she refuse him this one little thing?

'All right,' she said. 'We'll have dinner together one evening.'

'Tomorrow.'

'I'll talk to Hilda—'

'You'll do no such thing. You're the guest. Send Hilda up to talk to me about the menu. You go and pick out your prettiest dress to wear.'

She possessed nothing that could even remotely justify the title 'your prettiest dress'. Apart from her jeans and uniform she had one plain linen garment that was businesslike and totally unsuitable for the kind of evening he was suggesting.

Nor could she even hint that it didn't matter what she wore, because to say that would be to hurl his blindness at him.

'I don't have anything suitable with me,' she said at last. 'This kind of invitation doesn't usually come my way when I'm working.'

'Then you should buy something new, at my expense. Think of it as therapy for the patient. This means a lot to me.'

'Well, if you put it like that—'

'New dress—preferably long—shoes, hairdo. The works.'

She laughed. 'All right.'

'You'd better go into town right now. Go on with you. Oh, and Elinor—'

She stopped in the doorway.

Jason's grin was full of mockery for himself.

'*I'm sorry,*' he said.

It was the kind of carefree shopping expedition that had vanished from her life, and to be having one now, for

Jason Tenby's sake, seemed incredible.

Yet she knew exactly what she wanted. She'd looked through his blind eyes and seen the world that constricted him and drove him mad. And, no matter how strange it seemed, she would help him to imagine that he'd escaped, even if only for one evening.

She had clear ideas about what she was seeking—something that would be pretty enough for evening wear, yet also serviceable.

But then she walked past a small shop and stopped, transfixed. One window was dominated by a chiffon dress in shades of orange, brown, green and yellow. It was like sunrise and sunset. It was wine and laughter, earth, air and fire, and it sang to her of life and all that made life beautiful.

Doubtless there had been other dresses, but she hadn't seen them or heard the song. Just why it should have happened today, this minute, she didn't know, but inside her rose a passionate, irrational yearning for this one garment.

She went in, half hoping that it wouldn't fit, but it fitted to perfection. She had an eerie feeling that fate had seized her by the hand, although whether fate was acting for her or against her it was too soon to tell.

She had it on before she asked how much it cost. And when she heard the answer she gasped. The price was wicked, but so was the dress, and a little wickedness seemed delightful right now.

After that she seemed to have no say over her own actions. Carried away, she bought elegant evening sandals, and a froth of silk underwear. The shop was connected to a beauty salon next door, and it was easy to book an appointment for a hairdo and make-over for the following afternoon.

She returned to Tenby Manor, torn between guilt and delight. Her purchases were going to turn her into somebody else and suddenly she wanted that madly, recklessly. Oh, the joy of being someone else, just for a few hours!

But how would Jason react to the size of the bill?

He reacted by shouting with laughter. 'Boy, that must be some dress!'

'It isn't just for the dress,' she admitted. 'I bought a few other things.'

'Good. Tell me.'

'Some evening sandals, and tights…'

'And?' For her hesitant voice hinted at something more.

'And some underwear. I had to,' she added quickly, 'because the dress is a bit low and nothing I have is suitable—'

'Dragon Lady, you're blushing.'

'I'm not. Don't be absurd.'

'Your voice is blushing.' He added wickedly, 'Tell me about the underwear. I want all the details.'

'Well, you're not going to get them. If you feel I've wasted your money I shall be happy to pay for the extras myself.'

'By "extras" you mean bra and panties?' he asked with a grin.

'Yes. And a slip.'

'Satin?'

'Yes.'

'Colour?'

'Peach.'

'Does it all match?'

'Perfectly.'

'Sounds like money well spent to me,' he said happily.

'That's without my appointment tomorrow.'

'You really pushed the boat out, huh? Great.'

'I asked Hilda to make some tea. I'll go and see if it's ready.'

It was an excuse to flee the room. As Jason had mysteriously detected, she was blushing, and not just her face but her whole body. From head to toe she was suffused with warmth at the intimate images Jason had forced her to put between them.

He would never see the delicate, feminine underwear. Nor did he know what she looked like, so his imagination was curtailed. Yet she had the odd feeling that he could picture her exactly. It was as though he had the power to undress her, and it was very unsettling.

At the beauty salon next day she found that the staff knew she'd bought the dress in the window next door.

'It must be a very special occasion,' the stylist said as she examined her hair.

'Yes, I suppose it is.'

She rejected some of the fancier styles she was shown, and finally settled on a soft arrangement that left her shoulder-length hair hanging free but elegantly shaped.

The beautician was armed with an array of colours that complemented her dress. Elinor started out doubting, but all doubts vanished as she saw her new self.

It was a stranger who looked back at her, a ravishing, beautiful stranger, elegant to her fingertips. A desirable woman, who *knew* she was desirable. Elinor drew in her breath in wonder.

'One last little thing,' said the beautician.

She began to spray perfume lightly over Elinor's hair and neck. Elinor sensed its sultry yet subtle aroma. 'What is that?'

Laughing, the beautician told her the world-famous name.

'But that costs two hundred pounds an ounce,' Elinor gasped.

'Well, it's just a little sprinkle for a special evening. He won't be able to resist you.'

It was indeed a perfume for a woman who wanted to be irresistible: delicate, understated, haunting. Elinor was thrilled by it, yet she wished she wasn't wearing it tonight. It fitted the alluring underwear too well, as Jason would certainly know.

She was half afraid the vision would vanish when she put on the dress that evening. But when she saw the creature who looked back at her from the mirror she felt like Cinderella just before the ball.

Hilda was entranced. She'd entered into the scheme with gusto and had produced her best culinary magic. At least, so Elinor assumed. She hadn't been allowed in the kitchen since yesterday.

'I think it's wonderful what you're doing for him,' Hilda said when she'd helped lower the dress over Elinor's head without disturbing the hairdo. 'If only he could see you! It's heartbreaking that he's so pleased about tonight when he's going to miss so much of it.'

'Yes, it makes you realise how little he really has left,' Elinor sighed.

'I remember when he was taking a girl out to dinner in the old days,' Hilda said. 'Different one every night sometimes. That was before Lady Virginia of course.'

'Of course,' Elinor said demurely. 'Bit of a devil, was he?'

'Oh, more than a bit,' Hilda said admiringly. 'When he was a lad he was like one of them sultans, taking his pick of the harem. Never cared what anyone else thought. Except—'

'Except what?' Elinor asked curiously.

'Something happened a few years back. I'm not sure what, but it hit him hard, and after that he changed. He began to take more trouble about people's feelings. He was a bit brusque before.'

'Yes, I shouldn't think he was the imaginative type.'

'Oh, he'd always been kind. He'd do the right thing by people, but you had to take him as you found him. Suddenly he became gentler.'

'And you don't know what made him change?'

'No, love. I was in hospital, and then Jason paid for me to go to a convalescent home, so I was gone for a few months. There!' She stood back to admire. 'You're as pretty as a picture.'

Elinor had been ordered to stay away from the dining room while Hilda made her preparations. Now she approached it and found the door closed. She took a deep breath before knocking.

'Come in,' Jason called.

She did so, and stopped at the sight of him, sitting in the wheelchair. He was fully dressed in a black evening suit, smart black leather shoes, snowy white frilled shirt, with a black bow-tie. Diamond cuff-links winked at his wrists. Jason had turned out in style for her.

He'd had the room done up in style too. It was filled with the choicest blooms from the Tenby hothouses, and a traditional log fire burned in the old-fashioned fireplace.

The great table had been moved aside to make room for a small one, laid for two. Elinor's eyes widened as she recognised the china as the family's best Sèvres service. Beside each plate stood three wine goblets of heavy cut-glass crystal, each one worth a fortune.

She knew their value because she had seen all this before, on the night of the ill-fated dinner party. Jason had had it laid out then, just as now, ostensibly in her honour. And then he had destroyed her.

'Elinor?' he asked.

'Yes, I'm here.' She thrust the memory away. 'You've really pushed the boat out.'

'To do a lady honour,' he said gallantly. He indicated the table. 'Is it to your liking?'

'It's beautiful,' she said. 'The flowers…'

In a small vase by her place were a few bright yellow king cups, plucked from the wild. She was charmed.

He held out his hand and she placed hers lightly in it. Manipulating his wheelchair with one hand, he led her further into the room. She was aware of him listening for the soft rustle of her dress, and inhaling her softly seductive aroma.

'Tell me what you look like,' he said.

She described the autumn colours and the garment's silky texture and he nodded with pleasure.

Two aperitifs, ready-poured, stood on a small table. Jason positioned his chair and reached out for the glasses, finding them so exactly that Elinor guessed he'd been practising the move. He handed one glass to her and raised his own so that she could clink hers against it.

'To a pleasant evening,' she said.

'To the best evening I've had in months. Thank you for doing this, Elinor. It means a lot to me to feel human again.' He sniffed the air appreciatively. 'You certainly know how to choose a perfume.'

'That was an accident,' she said quickly. 'They sprayed it on in the salon, without asking me first.'

He frowned slightly. 'Does that matter?'

'It's just that it makes me feel a little odd, as though I were pretending to be something I'm not.'

He stirred. 'What made you say that?'

'What?'

'Pretending to be something you're not.'

Too late she remembered how he'd once thrown those very words at her.

'It's just a phrase,' she said lamely. 'I could have said anything.'

'Yes, I suppose so.' He seemed to be murmuring to himself. 'It's strange. Sometimes I seem to feel a ghost in this room.'

She managed to control her gasp, but she looked straight at him, riveted. She wondered if he could tell.

'Do you believe in ghosts?' he asked.

'Not dead ones,' she replied, picking up his thought.

'Nor me. But living ghosts, the echoes of people as they once were, who felt something so deeply that their feelings lingered in the air—'

'Oh, yes,' she said softly. 'I believe in them.'

'I thought you'd understand.' He seemed to pull himself together. 'Hilda has left the meal on a hot trolley. Would you mind doing the honours?'

He wheeled himself to the table, and Elinor began to serve him. As she finished he caressed the dress, nodding as if in pleasure at its soft silkiness. Then he reached up and laid his hands on her arms. His touch was light, but it seemed to burn her.

'Do you mind?' he asked.

She was shaken but she said, 'No. I've tried to look as you wanted.'

'May I go further up?'

She had a sense of danger, but she forced herself to say, 'Of course.'

She pulled up a chair close by him and touched his hand to indicate that she was ready. Inch by inch his hands slid up her arms, discovering her bare shoulders with the delicate straps that held up the dress. He found her throat, her long neck and clean jawline. Her hair swung softly against his fingers and he touched it with a concentrated look on his face.

'I'll stop if I'm offending you, Elinor.'

'You're not,' she said firmly. After all, this was only a kind of therapy, to raise the patient's spirits. But a pulse at the base of her throat had started to beat heavily, and she was afraid that he would detect it.

His gentle touch on her face unnerved her, especially when he traced the outline of her mouth, recalling the shocking moment when he'd done the same thing on the first night. Her heart was beating again as it had done then.

She tried to hold still and think of nothing, but she found her attention focusing on his own mouth. It was wide, firm-lipped and generous, and she could remember exactly how it had felt against hers, moving with persuasive seduction, teasing and inciting her until she'd started to kiss him back. She couldn't deny it, and the remembrance brought the blush back to her body. Any minute he would sense what was happening to her, and that mustn't happen. She tensed, and at once Jason drew back.

'I don't know what got into me,' he said. 'I suppose I shouldn't have done that.'

'It's all right, honestly.'

'You were trembling. I'm sorry.'

'No, don't be. And I'm not trembling. It's just that I'm not used to being dressed like this. It's a bit chilly around the shoulders. Let's start the meal.'

She seated herself opposite him. The table was so small that even with it between them they were still close.

'Thank you for making so much effort,' he said. 'You might have thought it wouldn't have made any difference, but it does. Not just the perfume, but the dress. I love the dress.'

She hardly knew what to make of him. The man she'd known long ago would never have behaved like this. She could only guess at the changes six years had made. She herself wasn't the same person. But perhaps this was his desperation talking. Once he hadn't known what it was to be in need of reassurance. Now he knew nothing else.

'I know that your inner pictures matter a lot,' she said.

'Yes. So help me out a bit more. Are you wearing all the other things?'

'I don't know what you mean,' she said primly.

His grin was wicked. 'Yes, you do.'

'Oh, the sandals!' she said with an air of innocence. 'Yes, I'm wearing them.'

It was sweet to tease him, and sweeter still to hear his chuckle as he said, 'I wasn't talking about the sandals, and you know it.'

'Then I don't know what you are talking about,' she said calmly, although she knew very well. With a twinge of dismay, mixed with delight, she realised that she was being sexually provocative, something so foreign to her that she was alarmed at how much she enjoyed it.

She had a moment's guilt about Lady Virginia, and banished it at once. If Jason's fiancée had bothered to be here he wouldn't have needed to seek diversion like this.

'I'm talking—as you know very well—about the peach satin slip, and the matching bra and panties.'

'Oh *them*!' she said with an air of surprise.

Jason laughed outright and reached for her across the table. She offered her hand and he carried it to his lips.

'Yes, them.'

'You don't need to know about them,' she said with an attempt at firmness.

'Why not?'

'Because I'm wearing a dress over them.'

'So I couldn't see them anyway,' he finished for her. 'Elinor, don't you understand? Even if I could see the dress, I'd still be sitting here trying to imagine you without it. Don't tell me no man has ever mentally undressed you before?'

Through the blush that engulfed her she managed to say, 'Certainly no one has ever sat there and told me about it before. You're disgraceful. Now let go of my hand, and let me serve you some food.'

He laughed again, and it wasn't the laugh of an invalid, but of a full-blooded man thinking full-blooded thoughts. Nor did he release her hand. Hilda's words came back to her; '…like one of them sultans, taking his pick of the harem…'

She smiled, wishing she could have known Jason in those days. Then the smile faded, as she remembered that she had.

In a moment the past came flooding back, overwhelming her, making her little Cindy Smith again. What was she doing here, creating fantasies with Jason Tenby?

Then she saw his face, smiling blindly up into hers, full of trust. The past vanished. She squeezed his hand.

'Do you want to eat or not?' she challenged him.

'In default of something else. Hurry up, woman! Serve a hungry man.'

She laughed and began to attend to the food.

CHAPTER EIGHT

WHEN their heaped plates were before them she tried to get things back on a more prosaic footing. 'I'm glad you approve of my choice of clothes, although it isn't a long dress, as you wanted.'

'Never mind. You'll find it more useful for going to parties.'

'That's true.'

'But I forgot. You don't go to parties.'

'Don't I?'

'You didn't have a suitable dress for this evening,' he reminded her.

'But I move around from job to job. I travel light.' He made a noncommittal reply and concentrated on his food. There was a scratching at the door and Elinor went to investigate. Bob immediately slithered in and went to crouch under the table. Despite their protests he refused to move away from the area of food.

It became a merry meal, with the little dog begging titbits and stuffing himself 'like a pig' as Jason trenchantly declared. Elinor was glad of his presence, which prevented the conversation straying into dangerous areas.

Not that she really wanted to prevent that. But she enjoyed the danger too much, and she was trying to stay professional.

But at last she put her foot down and ordered Bob from the room. It took another titbit to get him out of the door, but she finally closed it behind him, and returned, laughing, to the table. Jason too was grinning.

'I don't usually take him with me when I wine and dine a lady,' he complained. 'I blame you. Ever since you encouraged him into my room he's been impossible.'

'That's right, it's all my fault,' she agreed. She felt light-headed, and wondered if she'd had a little too much of the excellent wine.

'Let's sit down comfortably,' he said.

A small sofa stood by the fire. Jason turned the wheelchair towards it and she saw what he meant to do. She bit back the offer to help and was glad she'd done so when he managed to get himself out of the wheelchair and onto the sofa with another practised movement. He patted the place beside him, and she joined him.

'You sound different when you laugh,' he observed, cocking his head towards her slightly.

'So does everybody.'

'No, I mean something more. Most of the time you're holding yourself hidden from the world behind a locked door. But when you laugh the door opens. Not much. Just a crack, enough to be tantalising.'

She drew in a slow breath. How had this blunt, unsubtle man come so dangerously close to the truth about her? Was it just the sharpened insight of the blind, or had she always misunderstood him?

'What is it, Elinor? Why the long silence? Did I come too close to your secret?'

She made an effort at recovery. 'I don't have secrets.'

'No, no; that will do for Nurse Smith, but I didn't invite Nurse Smith to dinner. Talk to me—just as you would if I weren't blind.'

If you weren't blind you'd have thrown me out long ago, she thought.

'Do you know, after all these weeks, I don't even know where you were born?' Jason said.

This wasn't too difficult. She'd guessed he would probably ask about her background, and was ready.

'A country town, rather like Hampton Tenby,' she said. 'We lived in a small terrace back-to-back house.'

'Did you always want to be a nurse?'

'Yes, I suppose I did,' she said thoughtfully, refilling his glass. 'My father was often ''unwell''. That was how my mother put it when he staggered home and collapsed into bed. It was ages before I understood what ''unwell'' really meant.'

'Drinking?'

'Yes. I used to fuss around trying to make him better. He'd sleep it off, and wake sober, and I thought I'd cured him. Only he always became unwell again, and I thought it meant I was a failure.'

'Poor little girl,' Jason murmured. 'What a burden for a child!'

'When he was sober he was lovely, and I wanted him to be lovely all the time. But when I was twelve he fell into a ditch and passed out, and by the time they found him he had pneumonia. We went to see him in the hospital, but he died without coming round.'

'And you loved him,' Jason said gently.

'Yes, I did. I was too young to know how destructive drinking can be, and I was very unfair to my mother. I thought it was all her fault for not understanding him. Once—'

She stopped because a sharp memory had pierced her.

'Once?' Jason prompted.

'I was about ten. Mum and I were having an argument and I said, ''Why are you so nasty to Daddy?'' She just looked at me sadly and said, ''Please, love, don't say that.'' Then she went away and later I found her crying her heart out. *Oh Mum!*'

Jason heard her voice tremble and quickly put out his hand to find her. 'What is it?' he asked urgently. 'Are you crying?'

'It's just that—I haven't thought of it for years,' she choked. 'I was so unkind, and I made her unhappy. But I didn't understand—'

'How could you? You were a child. Don't be hard on yourself.'

'Oh, I know you're right. And of course I grew up and came to see how it had really been for her. She and I got on really well in the end. But I wish I'd told her I was sorry before she died.'

'She'd probably forgotten it too,' Jason suggested.

'I know, it's just—remembering how she cried—and it's too late.' She sighed and said wistfully, 'It's terrible to realise too late.'

'Yes,' he said quietly. 'It is.'

She wondered what had come over her. She'd never told that incident to anyone before, not even Simon. In fact, until tonight, she hadn't recalled it. But it had seemed natural to tell Jason, and even more natural that he had understood.

Too late—you vanished—' He'd said those words on the first night to some woman he hadn't named, but whom he'd kissed with a kind of despairing tenderness. He knew that 'too late' were the saddest words in the world.

'What are you doing?' he asked, hearing a clinking sound.

'Opening the last bottle of wine. Perhaps I shouldn't. Too much gives me a headache.'

'Then you've been drinking cheap plonk. This stuff won't hurt you. I had the very best brought up in your honour.' He held out his glass and she refilled it.

When she had cleared everything away she went to the windows.

'Before you close the curtains, tell me what you can see,' Jason said.

'It's dark, but there's a full moon. I can see the lake in the distance, and the avenue of oaks. I can even make out some lights in the valley.'

'It must look beautiful.'

'You'll see it again, Jason.'

'I never really bothered to look at it properly when I could. There was always so much to do, and no time to stand and stare. I'd give anything to be able to stand and stare now.'

There was nothing to say. She wouldn't protest any more in case he heard in her voice that she only half believed. He seemed to pick up so many subtle signals now that once he would have missed.

She returned to the sofa. She was feeling relaxed, and it was easy to answer when Jason said, 'How old were you when your mother died?'

'Seventeen. I did odd jobs for a while, then started my nursing training. Ever since I qualified I've done this kind of work because I like change.'

Jason frowned. 'Aren't you missing something out?'

'What—do you mean?' Elinor asked cautiously.

'Something about your voice has intrigued me since the first day.'

'What about my voice?'

'There was nothing in it, as though you'd carefully wiped all the life away.'

'That's my professional voice.'

'So I thought, but— All right, it's none of my business.'

'It certainly isn't,' she said tensely.

'Don't be mad at me. I thought we were becoming

friends, and you could tell me things. But you're right. I had no right to pry.'

'You're not. But there are things I can't tell you.'

'Who do you tell? Have you got anybody at all that you talk to?'

'No,' she said after a moment.

'Poor Elinor. You're stranded in a desert, just as I am.'

'You'll come out of your desert, Jason.'

'And when will you come out of yours?'

Suddenly the impulse to tell the truth was irresistible. 'Does it matter? A desert can be a very safe place.'

'For God's sake! You're not old enough to know that.'

'Jason, please forget this conversation. I don't know what made me say such a thing.'

'You said it because it's true. You opened that door a fraction, but you're slamming it again now, aren't you?'

'And suppose I am?' she said, growing angry and afraid. 'Why can't I keep some part of myself just for me and nobody else? Maybe I don't want to come out of the desert. Maybe I need it. Don't try to force me, Jason. Leave me where I feel safe.'

'I'm sorry,' he said at once. 'I had no right to demand your confidence. You've been very kind talking to me about yourself.'

He said the last words in a cool, formal voice that showed her what she'd done. Dismayed, she surveyed the wreck of an evening that had been so good until then.

'Jason, I—'

'I've enjoyed our dinner,' he said, in the same voice. 'Now perhaps it's time for it to end— *My God!*'

The last words were a shout. He jerked up straight, reaching for her wildly.

'What is it? I'm here.' She caught his flailing hands. 'Tell me what's happened.'

'My foot. It's got pins and needles. Do you hear that? *I've got pins and needles in my foot.*'

'That's marvellous. Are you sure?'

'Sure? It's driving me crazy, but it's wonderful. Elinor, I can feel something. Do you know what that means?'

'Yes, I know what it means,' she said, half laughing, half crying. 'It means the feeling's coming back to your legs.'

'And that means I'm going to walk again, right?'

'Yes—well, probably—it's a good sign.'

'Good? It's the most wonderful thing that's happened in months. Elinor, *Elinor!*'

The last word was a groan that was half triumph as he pulled her into his arms. She fell against him and his arms closed around her fiercely.

She gave one brief gasp of protest before her own response overwhelmed her, carrying away the nurse in the woman so quickly that she had no time to think. She could feel the power flowing through him. This was no longer an invalid, but a man returning to life and rejoicing in it.

His lips were skilful, telling her of ardour and longing, and inviting her to tell him the same. He pressed her eagerly against his heart while his mouth explored hers and she slowly turned into flame in his arms.

He might be helpless in the rest of his life, but his lips could still kiss a woman to madness, driving her and himself on with his passionate will. He was inside her mouth, exploring it with his tongue, teasing fire from her soft skin so that she moaned helplessly and clung to him.

Every part of her was alive, burning, wanting this to go on for ever. She felt the touch of his fingertips on her neck, her shoulder, her breasts, outlining her shape as though he was trying to sear it into his senses. She could sense his control slipping away, taking her own with it, thrilling her. At any moment…

'Jason—*no!*'

'*Elinor.*'

'No—let me go—*let me go*—'

Reluctantly he did so. He was gasping, like a man fighting to free himself from feelings that shook him to the core. Slowly he released her and she stood up, backing away from him.

She could see a woman in the mirror over the mantelpiece. Her hair, once so carefully dressed, was tumbling in disorder, her face was flushed with passion, her eyes bright with pleasure. One slender strap of her dress was displaced, as though she'd been about to toss her clothes aside and offer herself madly to the man. Her full breasts were rising and falling with the force of her sensations. She was wanton, she was ecstatic. She was herself.

She was glad he couldn't see what he'd brought her to. But he would sense. He would know, because it was the same with him, and no man in the grip of desire could mistake the woman's burning response.

At the same time she wished she could see the expression in his eyes. Would they reveal that he was as stunned as she felt?

'I'm sorry,' he said hoarsely. 'I had no right to do that. Dear God, what possessed me? Please—'

'You were happy,' she said hurriedly. 'And I'm happy for you. That—that was all.'

She saw him shudder and when he spoke again she could hear the effort to sound normal.

'It *is* good news, isn't it, Elinor?'

'It's the best. We're going to get there.'

They were both talking for the sake of it, making sounds while they hastily tried to put their relationship back onto a basis where they need not be embarrassed when they met next day.

'It's late; you should be in bed,' she said in a shaking voice. 'I'll clear the things away.'

She hastily piled dishes onto the trolley and wheeled it out to the kitchen. When she returned Jason had managed to get back into the wheelchair and was waiting at the foot of the stairs. Even in his blindness he had an air of triumph, and her heart contracted with tenderness for him.

At that moment she would have done anything, made any sacrifice, if only things could go well for him.

But she forced herself to be sensible as she took him upstairs and helped him into bed.

'Try to get a good night's sleep. I'll do some tests to-morrow, and we'll have a busy day.'

'Sleep? After the news I've just had? All right, all right. Anything you say, Dragon Lady.'

'Yes, well, I *am* a dragon lady, and don't you forget it.' She tried to find just the right note of brisk cheerfulness, afraid that her voice might be shaking.

She settled him for the night, trying to touch him as little as possible. She needed to be alone with her turbulent thoughts.

When the house was quiet Elinor slipped outside and walked under the stars. She was shaken to the core by what had happened. Her enemy had kissed her passionately and she had revelled in it. This wasn't like the kiss he'd given her in his sleep. This had been a full, red-blooded, all-male very determined kiss. And she had answered with fire.

She'd responded against her own will, but her will was like a twig swept away in a storm. She'd wanted Jason's kiss, and now she knew that a part of her had been waiting for it.

Because a door had opened in her mind, and through it she could glimpse the memories that she had been suppressing for six years.

That night in the library, Jason had forced his embrace on her to separate her from his brother. But at the first touch of his lips on hers she had felt a thrill such as she had never known before in her life. The pleasure she'd known in Simon's arms had been revealed for the pallid thing it was.

In those few blinding moments she'd discovered that real pleasure was being kissed by a man whose lips were fierce, urgent yet subtly seductive. She'd disliked and feared him, yet the purposeful movements of his mouth on hers had sent her into a spiral of ecstasy, and before she knew it she was responding.

He'd been as astonished as she was herself. She'd seen his eyes, amazed, heard him say her name on a new note, before the seductive assault had been renewed. And then she was kissing him back, saying his name mindlessly, wanting this to last forever.

And that was what Simon had seen.

In those few brief moments in Jason's arms she'd glimpsed passion as she'd never dreamed of it. Her body's uncontrollable response had been a betrayal of the man she was sure she loved. Jason had thrilled her as Simon never had and never could. And Simon had seen it. Which meant she'd deserved all the bitter words he'd hurled at her.

That was the truth, a terrible truth that for six years she'd buried so deep she'd forgotten where she put it.

And tonight, in his arms once more, the illusion had

finally been shattered. Jason Tenby wasn't only her enemy.

He was also the man she longed for with every fibre of her being.

She was in Jason's room early next morning, asking, 'How are the pins and needles?'

'Worse,' he said in a tone of fervent thankfulness. 'They're in both legs now. I'm feeling things again. Dear God, I thought it would never happen! I'll be walking in no time.'

'Jason, please don't get excited too soon. It's a very good sign, but walking will take some time yet. Let me test your reflexes, then I'll give Andrew a call.'

Her tests confirmed that the feeling was returning to his legs, and Jason's spirits soared. She didn't repeat her warning, but looked at him tenderly, praying he would be spared further disappointment.

There was still one hurdle to cross. As she was getting ready to go down to breakfast she remarked casually, 'If I'd known that wine was so potent I wouldn't have drunk so much.'

And he followed her lead, saying, 'I put away quite a bit myself. Did I behave intolerably?'

She actually managed to laugh. 'You behaved like a man who'd had wonderful news.'

'And to him all things are forgiven?' he asked lightly.

'There was nothing to forgive,' she assured him.

And so the truth was reinvented into a shape they could live with. A shape they could both see.

The time was soon coming when the mask would be removed from Jason's eyes. His optimism about his legs had convinced him that all obstacles could now be overcome, and he was eagerly looking forward to the day.

Elinor was less sure. She needed someone to talk to about Jason, and when Andrew called to invite her for a meal she accepted eagerly.

She slightly regretted it the next moment when he said, 'There's a new restaurant in town that does the best food and wine you've ever tasted.'

'Oh, no, a burger will do,' she assured him.

'Burger nothing. I'm entertaining you in style. Wear that new dress Hilda tells me is so ravishing.'

It dawned on her that Andrew saw this as a date. She'd been so preoccupied with Jason that she'd hardly thought of anything else. But she couldn't get out of it now without being rude, and it would still be a chance to talk about Jason.

'If it's all right with you I'll be out tomorrow evening,' she told Jason. 'I'm having a meal with Andrew.'

'I thought we were going to listen to the radio,' he said, a tad sharply. 'It's the last episode of *The Praying Mantis*.'

'Oh, dear, I forgot.'

She could have kicked herself. They'd listened to the serial together and squabbled about the murderer's identity. Not to be there for the denouement was like snubbing him.

'I'll call Andrew and change the date.'

'Nonsense. I won't fall apart because you have a night out.'

Andrew collected her the following evening. She'd just finished dressing and came down to greet him, before returning upstairs to finish her make-up. He waited for her in the study, with Jason.

'I've prescribed myself a medicinal whisky,' Jason said, holding up the glass. 'I won't offer you one because you're chauffeuring the most important person in my life at the moment.'

Andrew grinned. 'Don't let Virginia hear you say that.'

'That's quite different,' Jason said with a touch of constraint.

'Sure it is. I can't imagine my cousin haunting a sick room and soothing your fevered brow. How is Virginia these days, by the way? In London buying her trousseau, isn't she?'

'No, that was the original plan, but it's on hold for the moment,' Jason said stiffly. 'Where are you taking Elinor?'

'The Dandelion. Great place. Very plush. At least she'll have the proper setting for that dress I just saw her in. When I met her she was a wood nymph. Tonight she'll be a spirit of the forest.'

'Are you *on* something?' Jason demanded with the plain man's revulsion for flowery words.

'Just high on love,' Andrew assured him. 'How long is she going to be?'

On cue, Elinor opened the door. Jason heard the faint click of her shoes, then Andrew, saying, 'You look fantastic!'

Elinor laughed. 'Thank you.'

'That colour makes your skin glow,' Andrew went on fervently. 'Boy, will you turn heads!'

Out of sight Jason clenched his hands into fists. Why the devil didn't they both just go? He became aware of Elinor's perfume, fresh and haunting, reminding him of honeysuckle and roses, and all the good things of the earth.

'Are you sure you'll be all right without me this evening?' Elinor asked anxiously.

'Don't worry. Alf will haul me upstairs, and Hilda will put me to bed.'

'Yes, but—'

'Dragon Lady,' Jason said patiently, 'if the day ever dawns that I can't manage without you, I'll shoot myself.'

'Is that a yes?'

'That's a yes.'

'Hilda's here if you—'

'Clear off, the pair of you,' Jason said, half angry, half amused. 'Have a great time.'

Andrew laughed. 'Is my lady ready?'

'Quite ready, kind sir.'

Jason heard the creak of the door, the click as it was closed. He was alone again. From outside he heard Andrew's car driving away. Now he could let his hands unclasp.

Hilda came in to clear his supper things away.

'What did she look like, Hilda?'

'Oh, she was that pretty!' Hilda said enthusiastically. 'Tall and slender, and such long legs.' She gave an envious sigh. 'When I was a girl I yearned for legs like that. And that lovely silk dress, like trees in autumn.'

'He said it made her skin glow,' Jason murmured.

'That man is falling in love!' Hilda said sentimentally. 'It shines out of him. They'll be making a match of it soon.'

'You mean she's in love with him?' Jason asked casually. 'Surely not. She's only met him a couple of times.'

'He's only met her a couple of times,' Hilda pointed out. 'But he's nutty about her already. Why shouldn't she be in love? Nice young lady like that. Oh, they'll make such a gorgeous couple.'

'Splendid. Goodnight, Hilda.'

CHAPTER NINE

ELINOR was in no danger of falling in love with Andrew, but it was a long time since she'd had an evening out. She was a little taken aback to discover just how expensive the restaurant was. That made it a more intimate occasion than she'd wanted, but Andrew's manner was reassuringly light-hearted, and it seemed rude to make a fuss.

The dinner was delicious and Andrew put himself out to entertain her. What he lacked in looks he made up for in droll humour, and he soon had her chuckling.

'I'm glad you asked me out,' she said when the waiter delivered the wine. She was watching the level in the glass and so missed Andrew's alert movement of hope. 'It gives me a chance to talk about something away from Jason. I had an idea, and I need to know what you think about it.'

'Ah,' said Andrew, relapsing slightly.

She described Jason's first visit to the stables, and the subsequent visits they had made.

'I think it's done him a lot of good.'

'I'm sure of it,' Andrew agreed. 'It was a brilliant idea.'

'But he must long to be riding. We don't know if he'll ever walk, but even if he doesn't he could still ride.'

'Yes, I've heard about Riding For The Disabled schemes.'

'Don't let Jason hear you talk about him as "disabled"' Elinor warned. 'But I would like to find out a little more about it, so that when the time comes I can help him.'

127

'Can you ride yourself?'

'No,' she said briefly.

Andrew grinned. 'I wish you could see your face at this moment. I'll swear I touched a nerve. Go on, tell me what happened. Did you fall off a donkey?'

'Never mind. We're talking about Jason.'

'But I'd rather talk about you. Perhaps you should learn to ride. Jason lets me borrow his animals whenever I want. I can take one out, you come with me and I'll show you the ropes.'

'And he needn't know that I'm doing it for him,' she said eagerly. 'I don't want to say anything yet. It would depress him if he knew I was thinking about his future in those terms. Andrew, you're a marvel.'

He drew in his breath at the sight of her radiant face, her eyes glowing. Beautiful. Breathtaking. And none of it for him, he realised wryly.

'Of course, it shouldn't be me at all,' Elinor mused. 'Virginia should be here helping him. Doesn't she love him?'

'I'm sure she's fond of him, and he of her, but floating around a sick room isn't Virginia's style.'

'Is Jason her style? A man who may never make a complete recovery? Andrew, what do you think his chances are?'

'Elinor, I can't say that any more than you can. We'll know more when the mask comes off. Now, can we stop talking shop? I brought you out because I want to enjoy your company. Who wants Jason at the table as well?'

'I'm sorry,' she said, smiling. 'I just tend to get work on the brain.'

'You mean you're like this about all your patients?'

'Of course I am.'

'Hmm!' he said, regarding her askance.

The restaurant had its own small cabaret. Top of the bill was a local comedian. His jokes were old-fashioned but his delivery was masterly. They were still laughing on the way home.

'I'll take a last look at my patient before I go,' Andrew said, and mounted the stairs with her.

Suddenly Elinor was overcome with laughter again. She tried to stifle it but it burst out.

'What?' Andrew said.

'That woman in the audience,' she gasped. 'Do you remember what he said to her?'

'Yes, and her face.' He joined in her laughter, also doing his best to smother it.

'Shush, Jason might be asleep,' Elinor urged.

'No, there's a crack of light under the door.'

Hilda appeared in dressing gown and curlers. 'I waited up for you, love,' she whispered loudly. 'I thought you'd like a cup of tea.'

'Lovely,' Elinor said warmly.

Andrew slipped into Jason's room and found his patient sitting up by the window, listening to the radio. He switched it off and assumed a cheerful air.

'Did the evening go well?'

'It did and it didn't,' Andrew hedged.

'What does that mean?'

'It means that as far as I'm concerned I've found her. The one and only.'

'So when's the wedding?'

'There's an unexpected snag,' Andrew said, regarding Jason wryly.

'What kind of a snag? You don't mean there's already a man in her life?'

'Not officially, but I think I may have competition.'

'I wish you'd put it in plain words,' Jason said, annoyed.

'That's just what I can't do.'

'Stop being so damned mysterious!'

'Look, I didn't rush things. Take it slowly, no pouncing on the first date, that sort of thing.'

'I think you're very wise,' Jason said curtly.

'Are you feeling bad?'

'No, I've worked too much today, I suppose.'

Elinor came in with a tray of tea and three cups. 'You ought to be in bed,' she told Jason as she poured for him.

'So ought you,' he complained. 'Gadding about while your patient is abandoned.'

'Don't give me that abandoned stuff,' she riposted. 'Hilda loves you like a mother.'

He caught the unfamiliar, relaxed note in her voice, and frowned a little. He'd heard them climb the stairs and pause on the landing, smothering their laughter, and wondered if this was the Elinor Smith he knew.

The next ten minutes seemed like an age. It had never occurred to him before that his friend had so much meaningless small talk, but Andrew chattered on and on, and Jason thought he would never go. At last he threw good manners to the winds and gave a pronounced yawn.

'You'd better go, Andrew,' Elinor said. 'My patient needs his sleep and it *is* past midnight.'

'Yes, it is,' her patient agreed with meaning.

'Shall I help you into bed?' Andrew asked.

'I'm not ready for bed yet.'

'But you just said—'

'Goodnight, Andrew.'

'Goodnight, you old dog!'

Jason heard Andrew laugh, then the sound of a kiss, and finally the door closing.

The sound of a kiss.

'Did you have a good evening?' he asked.

'Oh, yes,' she said, with a sigh of pleasure.

'I believe Andrew's a very good host,' Jason observed, a mite too casually.

'The very best,' she said innocently. 'He makes me laugh.'

'So I heard as you were coming up the stairs.'

'We didn't wake you, did we?' she asked anxiously.

'Certainly not.'

How the hell did she think he'd managed to sleep while she was out until all hours?

'So come on, tell me,' she said.

'Tell you what?'

'About The Praying Mantis. Whodunit? Was it the husband or the cousin from Australia?'

'It was the cousin,' he admitted. 'You were right all the time.'

'Of course I was,' she said provocatively. 'Anyone would have known that.'

'You're fired.'

'Again? How many times is that?'

'I've lost count.' He yawned.

'It really is time you were in bed.'

'All right.' He wheeled himself over to the bed and swung around into the right position.

'Can you manage?' Elinor asked. Jason had developed a movement which involved half throwing himself from the chair into the bed, although he couldn't always manage it, especially if he was tired.

'Not tonight,' he said. 'I guess I should have let Andrew help me. Do you mind?'

'Of course not.'

She stood before him and leaned down so that he could

hold her shoulders. She clasped his body and straightened up. The feeling unnerved her. It was too sweet to hold him. She wanted to pull him closer and raise her face to his, but she mustn't because he belonged to another woman, because he was ill and trusted her, depended on her. It had never been so hard to be professional.

'Has your evening left you with enough energy to give me a massage?' he asked.

'Of course. Turn over.'

He tossed aside his pyjama jacket and lay waiting for the feel of her hands. They were like no others, he thought, soft and gentle, yet with the strength to soothe not only his body but also his mind. Her touch on his skin was a pleasure.

'Is that all right?' she asked.

'Go a bit lower. I've been aching all down my spine this evening.'

'Funny; that doesn't usually happen.'

'It's because you went away and left me,' he joked. 'The minute you're not there I go to pieces.'

She drew her hands down the length of his spine, trying not to be aware of his beauty. It was hard to stay detached when she was pervaded by tenderness.

And something more than tenderness, if she was honest. She was his nurse, and it was disgraceful that she took such pleasure in touching him, contemplating him. And it was alarming that all the years of stern discipline were no help to her now. The forbidden thoughts persisted in dancing through her mind, making her body glow.

She'd resolved to forget his kisses, but they wouldn't let themselves be forgotten. They were there on her lips this minute, reminding her of how it felt to want a man to distraction, to be alive and eager for love.

She was swept by an almost irresistible impulse to lay

her cheek against that smooth, muscular back, and touch it softly with her lips.

'That feels nice,' Jason grunted.

Shocked, she came back to reality, and realised that while she'd been dreaming the strong movements of her hands up and down his spine had softened until they were almost caresses. She pulled herself together and began to massage firmly again, until he said, 'Ouch!'

'Sorry,' she said hurriedly.

'By the way, I've got something to tell you.'

A hint of suppressed triumph in his tone alerted her. 'Jason—?'

'I spilt some hot tea on my legs tonight. And I felt it.'

'That's wonderful. Oh, and to think I wasn't here!'

'Yes, I'd have liked to share it with you at the time. But I dare say you'll soon be leaving anyway if you're going to let Andrew sweep you off your feet.'

'Don't be silly. We spent the evening talking about you.'

She finished her work and he rolled over so that his face was turned to her. 'And I suppose I didn't hear him kiss you?' he challenged.

'Only on the cheek. Just being polite. Now will you stop talking nonsense and go to sleep?'

He gave her a smart salute.

'Yes, Nurse! No, Nurse! Three bags full, Nurse!'

She laughed and the hairs on the back of his neck stood up. The soft whisper of her dress as she moved made them stand up again. He heard the door click softly behind her.

He knew he'd behaved disgracefully. He'd used a low-down trick as an excuse to hold her in his arms, and it had been as beautiful as he remembered.

Had she seen through it? Had she heard his heart hammering as he'd felt her slim body pressed close to his and let his cheek linger against her soft face? The memory of that flooded over him now, filling him with joy. He ought to be ashamed of himself. But he wasn't.

He lay back in the darkness, his hands behind his head, smiling. The feeling was returning to his body, and not just to his legs. Tonight he could dare to think of love again, as he hadn't dared for months.

And, to complete his happiness, Andrew had only kissed her on the cheek.

'Got the papers?' he asked when they were breakfasting in the conservatory next day.

'All of them. Where shall I start?'

'Skip the headlines; I've heard the news on the radio. I'm in the mood for something light.'

'Right.' She flicked through the pages. 'What shall it be? The funnies? The comment? The society column? Lord Who has eloped with Lady Whatever and they're—'

'What is it?' Jason asked, curious about her sudden silence.

'I— Nothing, I dropped the newspaper,' Elinor said hurriedly.

'No you didn't. I'd have heard. What is it, Elinor?'

'All right,' she said reluctantly. 'There's a picture of Lady Virginia in the society column.'

'Who is she with?' Jason asked shrewdly.

'Freddie Sutherland,' Elinor said, reading. 'Apparently he's a millionaire with a house in Mayfair and an apartment in New York. Recently divorced.'

'And you think Virginia is aiming to become the next Mrs Sutherland?'

'Well—they're dancing very close. Still, I don't suppose that means anything. I expect she dances with a lot of people.'

'She was involved with Freddie at one time, but he married someone else. She hasn't been in touch for a while.' There was a sudden withered look about his face. 'The one kind of writing I can still read is the writing on the wall,' he said quietly.

'Oh, Jason, I'm sorry.'

He was very pale. 'Would you mind leaving me alone for a while? And don't let anyone else in.'

She slipped out and headed for the kitchen to warn Hilda. But at the last moment she looked back to the conservatory and saw Jason clench his hands, raising them as high as his head before slamming them down hard on the table. Then he raised his fists again, but this time he pressed his forehead against them.

'Damn her!' Elinor raged in the kitchen. 'Damn her for a heartless—'

'Whatever's happened?' Hilda asked.

'Lady Virginia is gallivanting in London with Freddie Sutherland, millionaire and playboy,' Elinor said, speaking almost savagely and making Hilda stare. 'How dare she?'

'Does Jason know?' Hilda asked anxiously.

'It was on the society page and I let it slip before I could stop myself. Oh, I could kill that woman!'

'How's he taking it?'

'He wants to be left alone, and I saw him— Oh, God! How can she do this to him?'

'Now, then, it won't help Jason if you upset yourself.'

'I'm not upset!'

'Why are you crying?'

'I'm not. Well, just a little.' Elinor blew her nose, furious with Virginia, and with herself.

She stormed out again and strode fast through the grounds until she came to the oaks. She leaned back against a mighty tree, trying to come to terms with the startling pain in her breast.

She flattened her hands against the bark, and her fingers encountered some letters carved there long ago. Looking down, she saw an S and a C intertwined—Simon and Cindy—just visible but very faded. Like the love itself.

How sweet and poignant the feeling had been once! And how faint it was now beside this new feeling that was struggling for recognition.

She'd got everything wrong. Oh, how wrong she'd been! Because Jason had shrugged off Virginia's absence she'd fooled herself into thinking he didn't care. But his fiancée's infidelity had devastated him. Elinor wished she hadn't seen him slamming his fists down, then burying his face against them. It was the gesture of a man in despair, torn in two by the defection of the woman he loved.

So why should she care whom Jason Tenby loved? She was his nurse, here to cherish and care for him, to heal him if she could. But not to love him.

She turned to the tree and hid her face in her arms.

After an hour Jason sent for her.

'We need to talk,' he said when he heard her in the conservatory doorway.

She came and sat down beside him. His face was deathly pale, and her pain increased.

'I called Virginia. Her engagement to Freddie will be announced any day.'

'I'm so sorry,' Elinor said desperately.

'Don't be. Something like this was bound to happen. I'm not heartbroken, Elinor. I've never been in love with her.'

'Please, Jason, there's no need to pretend. I saw how upset you were—'

'Yes, I was, but not about Virginia. We found it convenient to marry, but I didn't love her.'

'You didn't?' she asked breathlessly.

'Nor did she love me. And only a woman terribly in love could tie herself to a blind cripple.'

'Don't talk about yourself like that,' she said passionately.

'Why not? It's true. I should have faced it earlier, instead of waiting for her to tell me I'll never be a man again.'

'She said that?' Elinor demanded, outraged.

'Not in words. In fact she said all the right things. But actions speak louder. She doesn't want to waste any more time on me. And she's right.'

Elinor could hardly speak for anger. If Virginia had been there at that moment she would have wreaked vengeance on her for striking another blow at this man who was already staggering under so many.

'But you have things going for you,' she said urgently. 'You'll probably walk again—'

'And see?'

'I don't know,' she sighed.

'The doctor who treated my eyes was brilliant. But even she had to admit that there's a less than fifty per cent chance that I'll see again. And what are my legs without my eyes?

'It's strange how much is clear behind this mask. I can picture myself as the world does. That's what upset me: seeing myself through Virginia's eyes, as a man that any sensible woman would run a mile from.'

Elinor struggled to speak but her emotion was choking her. Jason's despairing acceptance hurt her as his hostility had never done. She wanted to enfold him in her arms and vow to protect him from the world's pain, but she knew that would be the worst thing she could do. It would merely underline his crippled condition.

'You've tried to reassure me,' he said quietly. 'Perhaps the best help you could give me now is to teach me to endure whatever I have to.' He turned a ravaged face to her. 'Can you do that?'

Once before she had reached this point, and backed off, refusing to tell him something that might help, because it would have hurt her too much to speak about it. But now all other pain faded beside his. Nothing mattered but to show him that here was a friend who'd known despair.

'Perhaps I can,' she whispered. 'You said once that I understood—and I do.'

'Tell me. For if ever I needed your help I need it now.'

'Something happened to me—long ago—that destroyed me. At least, that's how it felt—'

She broke off. It was hard, but the sight of Jason contemplating the wreck of his life made her go on.

'I lost the thing I cared for more than anything in the world,' she said at last, 'and lost it in a way I still can't bear to remember. I went away and hid where nobody knew me, and cried and cried and cried. And when I stopped crying, I found something strange.'

'What had happened?'

'Nothing. Absolutely nothing. The rest of the world went on as though I hadn't cried a single tear. It doesn't make any difference, you see, weeping and protesting—'

'Giving in to bitterness,' he supplied, with a touch of self-mockery.

'Yes. It's all just a stage you must go through before you realise that it's for ever, and you have to live your life on new terms. I still hope that it won't be for ever with you, but if it is—'

'Go on,' he said gently.

'I thought everything was over for me. It didn't seem possible that anyone could feel such misery and still live. I did, of course.' She took a deep breath. 'Only it wasn't me any more. It was somebody stronger who looked at everything differently. And she knew that life was still possible.'

'I suppose it was a man who did all this to you?'

'Yes.'

'But girls have painful love affairs all the time. There's always someone else.' When she didn't answer he said, 'I'm sorry, that was crass. It wasn't like that for you, was it?'

'No, it wasn't like that. I didn't actually decide not to love another man. But after a few years I discovered I'd turned into a woman who couldn't love.'

'Don't say that about yourself,' he said urgently.

'I can still see and talk and walk, but I've often felt as though part of me was missing. You can learn to live, Jason. You really can.'

'But is the life you have worth living?'

'I have a great deal—my work and a place in the world. It isn't the place I wanted, but it's a good place.'

'But that's not what I asked. Still, I suppose you've given me the answer.'

She didn't say anything. After a moment he squeezed her hand, and felt her squeeze softly back.

Strolling in the garden that evening, Elinor looked back at the house, at the light in Jason's bedroom window.

She'd half lied to him that day, telling him that she could never love again. She'd had to say that. If her words were to help him he needed to know that she understood a maimed life.

But that wasn't the real reason. There was another that she hardly dared to recognise.

She'd renounced love, but it had waited to pounce out of the darkness, catching her unprepared and forcing her to recognise it before she could marshal her defences. After six years her wayward heart had chosen this moment to be reborn. Like all births it was a kind of agony, but behind the pain was the promise of infinite joy.

CHAPTER TEN

TRUE to his word Andrew arrived one day ready for riding. Jason was settling in for a morning with Miss Horton and merely smiled when Elinor said she was going out for an hour or two.

She found herself mounted on Tansy, the slow, affectionate mare Jason had told her about. Andrew had brought her a hard hat, and under his excellent instruction she grew in confidence.

'You're doing well,' he told her on the second day.

'She's such a darling,' Elinor said, patting Tansy's neck. 'She never does anything to scare me.'

'Well, she's not going to set the world on fire, but she's dead right for you to ride with Jason. He won't be going very fast for a while. Still, at least he'll walk again.'

'But if he could only have one thing back he'd choose his eyes.'

'We'll know soon, but I'm afraid the chances aren't all that great.'

Elinor planned to mention her riding lessons later that day, but she hadn't allowed for the Tenby grapevine, which operated through Hilda, whose nephew worked in the stable. Slightly to her surprise Jason was annoyed.

'I wasn't deceiving you,' she said indignantly in answer to his curt remark. 'I'm planning for the day when you can take your first ride, and I didn't bother you with it because you were busy. Why make a mountain out of a molehill?'

'You're supposed to be here when I want you, not slipping off for secret trysts.'

He regretted the words at once. They were absurd and he knew it, but the thought of her seeking Andrew's company—on whatever pretext—riding and laughing with him beneath the trees, destroyed his sense of proportion.

'Secret trysts!' Elinor said in outrage. 'I've been studying a way to be more useful to you. And why shouldn't I see Andrew?'

'I can't think of a single reason,' he said crisply. 'Now, can we let it drop?'

'Certainly!' she snapped, feeling thoroughly ruffled.

But he knew he'd transgressed, and the next moment he gave her his most charming smile. 'I'm sorry, Elinor.'

'So you should be,' she said, but in a friendly tone that told him all was forgiven. 'I was going to tell you about Andrew. He's been giving me riding lessons, so that I can come out riding with you.'

'Fine, we'll go now!'

'You'll go when the dragon lady says so,' she said, smiling tenderly at his eagerness. 'And that won't be until your legs are a bit stronger. It's time you tried a few steps. I had a Zimmer frame delivered here this morning.'

'A what?'

'It's steadier than crutches. It'll be a lot of help in the beginning.'

'Then let's start right now,' he said eagerly.

In the privacy of his room he ran his hands over the frame. When he'd got the sense of it he said, 'Ready to go.'

She helped his feet onto the floor and stood at the other side of the frame, with her hands under his arms.

Taking a deep breath, Jason hauled himself up out of the wheelchair, letting his legs bear his weight for the first time in weeks. The sensation was alarming, dreadful. He gasped with shock and fought for control.

'My legs are like jelly; I can't—'

'Yes, you can,' she said quickly, wrapping both arms around him.

Instantly he rested one of his arms about her shoulders. 'I feel safer like this.'

'Good. Any way it feels right.'

'Shall we dance?' he asked, making a valiant try for a joke.

'We will dance together, I promise you.'

A look of fierce concentration came over his face.

'I can't move.'

'Give it time. Get used to being on your feet first.'

'All right. Let's just stand like this.'

But it wasn't a good idea. Jason's health and strength had returned, and at this distance there was no escaping his vibrant masculinity, or the warmth from his body pressed against her own. He was holding her far closer than necessary, and she guessed that if she could have seen his eyes she would have found a mischievous glint in them. How could she behave professionally, she thought wildly, when he made it so difficult?

'I—think that's enough for today,' she said in a shaking voice.

'But I'm quite happy as I am,' he said wickedly. 'You don't mind me leaning on you, do you?'

'Not at all,' she said, with an attempt at primness. 'It's my job.'

'The hell with that! You know what I mean.'

'Behave yourself!'

'Yes, Dragon Lady.'

'And don't call me that.'

'Stop me,' he teased.

'Oh, well, anything that cheers up the patient.'

He put his lips to her ear so that his warm breath tickled her. 'Shall I tell you what would cheer me up right now?'

'I don't think you should,' she said, trying to ignore the delightful images this evoked. 'In fact I think you ought to sit down now.'

'Not until I've taken a few steps.'

'All right. I'll push the frame out a bit ahead of you, and we'll put your hands on it—like that. Let it take your weight—steady—one foot forward—'

Slowly, inch by inch, Jason dragged one foot in front of the other, and then again. His teeth were gritted, sweat stood out on his forehead, but he made it.

'Did you see that?' he shouted.

'Yes,' she cried, laughing and crying. 'You did it! Oh, Jason, you did it!'

'Where are you?' He found her and held onto her in triumph. *'We* did it!'

'All right,' she said, feeling light-headed. 'Now for pity's sake sit down before your legs give out.'

'I think I'll lie down, and you can give them a massage.'

Carefully they made their way to the bed. He was tiring, and she could feel almost his whole weight on her shoulders.

'You're so frail,' he said. 'How can you hold me up?'

'I'm strong enough for whatever you need,' she said, feeling overwhelmed by happiness.

'Strange how I don't mind leaning on you. Once I would have hated it, but now it feels natural. Could we have met before?'

She froze with shock. 'Met—before?'

'In another life, perhaps. Maybe that's why I feel I've

known you for years. I wonder what we were once—friends, enemies, something else?'

She took a deep breath. This was very dangerous territory.

'It's not like you to be fanciful,' she hedged, playing for time.

'You bring out the fanciful in me. In fact you make me many things I never was before. Why is that, I wonder?'

Now she *must* tell him the truth, for if she passed up this chance the time would come when he would remember, and think the worst.

'Jason—'

She struggled for the words but, absorbed in him, she failed to notice the edge of a small rug. The next moment Jason had caught his toe on it and lost his balance. She fought to hold onto him, but he was too heavy, and they fell helplessly onto the bed, laughing, gasping, clinging to each other.

'Sorry about that,' Jason said, not sounding sorry at all.

'No, I'm sorry; I should have noticed that rug.'

He made no attempt to release her.

'Sometimes I care about being blind more than at other times. If only I could see your eyes now, I'd know if you want me to kiss you or not.'

What I want is to get up and get on with my job. The sensible words lined up behind her lips, all ready to be said.

And then they died. As she lay there in Jason's arms, feeling the soft thunder of his heart against hers, no power on earth could have made her sensible.

'You don't need eyes to know that, Jason.' Her voice was soft and teasing, as if it belonged to another woman, one who was at ease in the arms of the man she loved, who revelled, luxuriated in it. Not prim Nurse Smith, surely?

His face bore a sudden alert look. His hands on her arms tensed.

'How would I know, Elinor?'

'Like this,' she whispered, laying her mouth softly over his.

After the first movement of surprise he lay there and let her kiss him, savouring the pleasure. For once the darkness wasn't something to be feared, for *she* was darkness, and warmth and sweetness. Her body pressed against his was darkness, and her lips and tongue were darkness, teasing and inciting him. And the darkness was beautiful, because it was her.

'Do you think you understand now?' she murmured.

'Ask me again later,' he said shamelessly. 'I may take a lot of convincing.'

She laughed against his lips, and it destroyed his control. His arms went fiercely about her, so that her body lay along the length of his. He had just enough sensation to experience her pressed against him, and to appreciate that her body was beautiful. He ran his hands down over her waist, the swell of her hips, relishing her firm, youthful contours.

He knew he would regret it. He was tormenting himself uselessly with what couldn't be his—not yet, anyway, he amended hopefully. But physical pleasure had been denied him for too long, and now something in him was running riot at having this special woman in his arms, wanting her, and the growing, delightful awareness that she wanted him.

He tried to roll over so that she would lie beneath him on the bed. But his hips and thighs hadn't the strength yet, nor sufficient feeling. There was only feeling enough to know that he passionately desired this woman, and that not being able to do much about it was driving him mad.

'Damn!' he growled.

'What's wrong?' she murmured, reluctant to leave the lovely moment behind.

He breathed hard. 'Everything is wrong. I can't bear to kiss you like this if I can't—' His chest was rising and falling rapidly. 'How long before I'm normal?' he demanded raggedly.

'That depends how hard you work at it.'

'Get the crutches. Get me on horseback. Start by getting that frame back over here.'

'Not now. I'm going to massage your legs.'

'I'm not sure I can stand that,' he said, part humorous, part desperate.

'Never mind. The time is coming.'

The time when they would know whether he could see, when he would be back on his feet, functioning normally as a man: the time when he would know how much he had to offer her, and she must find an answer.

In the days that followed Elinor realised that they had slipped past another milestone. Now they were in a new country, where feelings could be taken for granted, and neither needed to speak of what they both understood.

Being Jason, he threw himself into the effort to walk with everything in him. He quickly dispensed with the frame and pushed himself to the limit on the crutches. More sensation was returning all the time.

'How's your horse riding now?' he asked one evening. 'Think you're good enough to protect me?' He spoke these last words with a grin.

'I'll give it a try,' she said. 'But it's too soon for Damon. You'll have to ride Rosie, in a built-up saddle.'

'Which I've no doubt you've already ordered.'

'It's been waiting in the stable for days.'

They went out next morning, and with the aid of a mounting block he made a better job of getting into the saddle than she'd expected. The stable lads clapped and Jason grinned an acknowledgement, while Elinor mounted Tansy. And then they were off, out of the yard and across the lawn towards the trees.

'How does it feel?' she asked after a while.

'Great, considering I can't see where we're going! I can't control Rosie with my legs, but she's such a peaceful soul that it doesn't matter.'

When they'd ambled for a while he said, 'Let's head for the stream. There's a place near the little bridge where there's a tree stump. If we use it as a mounting block, you can help me off.'

She found the spot, dismounted and tied up her horse. She climbed onto the stump and steadied Jason while he dismounted. When he was sure of his balance he stepped down to the ground, holding her with one hand and Rosie with the other. But instead of sitting down he leaned back against the trunk of a nearby oak tree and tightened his arm about her waist.

'If I die for it I'm going to kiss you on my own two feet,' he said, drawing her close.

She knew what he meant as soon as their lips touched. The confidence surging through him gave his mouth a new purpose, and with every fierce, skilful caress he was telling her that his days as an invalid were numbered and she would soon have him to reckon with. The thought of that time sent a thrill through her and she kissed him back ardently.

Problems fell away. This was the man she loved, no matter what strange paths had brought her to him. She loved him and she would tell him so in everything but words. Words were too perilous just yet.

But there were secrets that could be told all the more honestly for being silent. He sensed them in her eager response, and wondered what kind of woman this was who protected him like a lioness one moment, and melted in his arms the next.

'Stop, I can't breathe,' she protested.

'I don't want you to breathe,' he growled. 'I want you to forget everything but me—'

'I always—'

'Not as a patient, as a man. Don't you understand, or shall I kiss you again to make it plain?'

'No,' she gasped, 'Jason, please—'

He ignored her, kissing her ruthlessly until her head whirled. The lion was stirring again, telling her to beware because his strength had returned, and with it his authority. He was breathing hard when he released her.

'Why can't I see your face?' he grated. *'Why?'*

'You soon will,' she promised. 'The day after tomorrow.'

'And if I don't?'

There it was—the thought that haunted every moment with dread. In two days Andrew would come to uncover his eyes, and they would know his fate. Then his life would begin again, or he would be plunged into wretchedness.

'Suppose I can walk but not see?' he said. 'Wouldn't that be a sick joke?'

'Don't run to meet it,' she begged. 'Somehow we have to survive until then.' He was still holding her. Forgetting passion, she laid her head against his shoulder as though it were she, not he, who needed comfort.

'I'll try not to be a pain in the neck,' he promised, finding the top of her head and kissing it.

'You be as much of a pain as you like,' she said. 'That's what I'm here for.'

'Would you like me to tell you what you're here for?' he growled. 'No, perhaps not. That wouldn't help me keep calm. Give me a chaste peck and I'll try to think pure thoughts. It'll be hard, but I'll try.'

It thrilled her when he hinted at the urgency of his desire, and she couldn't help giving a soft, delighted chuckle. Sweat stood out on his brow.

'Don't laugh like that, Dragon Lady. Not unless you want me to lose my sanity.' He shuddered and pulled himself together. 'Now help me climb back on Rosie. And behave yourself.'

Elinor awoke so suddenly that she sat up before she realised it. She held still, straining to hear any noise from Jason's room.

It was the last night before the big day, and they'd both been on edge for hours. Now instinct told her that he was lying awake. She slipped across the corridor into his room.

'Can't you sleep either?' came his voice from the darkness.

'I dozed, but I woke up and felt sure you needed me.' She went to sit beside him on the bed.

'You must have heard me thinking about you,' he said. 'Tomorrow—it's what I've wanted and yet— The next few hours are going to be the worst of my life, but I can face them with you beside me.'

'I'll be here as long as you want me,' she promised.

'That might be a long time,' he murmured, almost to himself.

'What?'

'Nothing. I didn't say anything.'

His hand grasped hers tightly, as though she was all he had to cling to. She clasped him back, trying to offer him all the strength and courage she possessed.

'Stay with me,' he whispered. 'Don't leave me alone tonight.'

'I won't. Go to sleep.'

She watched him, feeling a passionate, tender protectiveness. At last she could tell by his breathing that he'd fallen asleep, and she raised his hand and held it first against her breast, then against her cheek.

After a moment she made a decision. Slipping off her dressing gown, she crept in under the covers to be with him. Deeply asleep though he was, he seemed to know she was there, and came into her arms at once. She held him close, resting her cheek against his head, possessed by an aching sweetness that made her want to weep.

Jason had said that only a woman 'terribly in love' could stick by him. With Simon love had been idyllic for a while, but Jason was a diffcrent man who needed her in a different way. With him love was poignant, joyful, sad, devastating and terrible. It was a fierce emotion, part desire, part tenderness, and it left her nowhere to hide.

And yet the problems lay in wait. If he regained his sight he would recognise her and demand an explanation. If he stayed blind and wanted her, she would still have to tell him the truth. Would he understand her innocent deception?

He stirred, but only to burrow against her a little more deeply, hiding his face between her breasts, inciting desires that tortured her. She wanted him so much.

It took only a moment to slip off her nightdress and offer him the full beauty of her naked body. He seemed to understand, for his hands began to explore her, while he murmured incoherent words of passion and longing. Her flesh, which for too long had been cold and unresponsive, came to burning life under his touch. No other man could have made her feel such sensations. Not even Simon—long in the past—had given her the pleasure she felt in Jason's intimate caresses.

He too was returning to life, becoming again a man who could love with his body as well as his heart. What she was doing now was dangerous, but no power on earth could have kept her from the rapt contemplation of his body beneath her hands, his limbs entwined with hers.

Perhaps this bittersweet moment was a kind of stealing, but she was like a beggar, hoarding crumbs. And she would steal those crumbs if she had to, in case they were all she ever had. If she had to leave and never see him again, she would still have this one night when she had been his, all his. Not a nurse, but a woman making a gift of herself, heart, soul and body, to the man her heart adored. And even if he never knew she would know, and treasure her secret.

She drew him closer, murmuring soothing words to prevent him awakening. She felt him relax against her, seeking refuge in her warmth.

'I'm here,' she whispered. 'I'm here, my darling.'

Andrew was on time. Everyone at Tenby Manor was agog, but Jason stayed upstairs, hidden from curious eyes, in case of the worst.

Jason greeted Andrew with a cheerful word but he was deadly pale. 'Let's get on with it.'

Andrew proceeded to ease the black mask off. But Jason didn't move, not even to open his eyes. Elinor watched him, not daring to breathe. Surely something must happen soon? But he sat, motionless, until he dropped his head. She understood then. He was afraid of the final step, afraid of the death of hope.

She dropped to her knees beside him.

'Jason,' she said softly, taking his hands gently in hers. 'Jason, it's all right. I'm here. Look at me, my dear.'

A violent tremor went through Jason, but he let her draw his hands down.

'Look at me,' she repeated. 'Open your eyes.'

'I can't,' he said hoarsely.

She touched his face with gentle fingers. 'You once said it drove you mad not to know what I looked like. Now's your chance to find out. It'll be all right. Trust me.'

Oh, God, she thought, *don't let me be wrong, or how will he bear it? How can I help him then?*

'You're not afraid, are you?' she asked. 'Not you?'

'I have no courage now except what you give me.'

'Then take what I have to give. Let me help you across the last hurdle.'

He raised his head and turned it to face her. Slowly he opened his eyes, but then instantly closed them again with a groan, threw his head back and covered his face with his hands.

'Oh, no!' Elinor wept. 'Please, no!'

'The light,' he cried. 'I can't bear the light.'

It was a moment before the truth dawned on her. She covered her mouth, almost choking with joy.

'He hasn't seen for a long time,' Andrew observed, smiling broadly. 'The light's going to be harsh just at first, plus it'll take a moment for him to focus.'

At last Jason looked down to where she was kneeling beside his chair, and a slow smile spread over his face.

'Elinor,' he whispered, 'you're beautiful.'

'Oh, Jason, Jason—' She hardly knew that her tears had begun to fall. He took her face between his hands. His eyes were clear and shining. And they held a look, as they gazed on her, that made her heart stop.

'Thank you,' he said simply. 'Thank you for getting me through this. For being there in the darkness—and now in the light. For being beautiful. For being as I dreamed of you. For being you.'

He laid his lips on hers. Elinor put her arms about his neck, and gave herself up to his gentle kiss.

With a sigh of resignation Andrew slipped out of the door. Neither of them knew that he'd gone.

'You can see,' Elinor said in wonder. 'Tell me that you can see.'

'I can see as well as I ever did.'

'Oh, thank God!' she whispered passionately. 'Thank God!'

She was dizzy. Everything was happening too fast.

By some mysterious process she'd felt Jason's pain as her own. And now his joy too was her own. She smiled up into his eyes, feeling the world rock beneath her.

At last she noticed that Andrew was no longer there, and in the same moment they heard a faint cheer from down below.

'Andrew must have told everyone,' she said. 'They all came to wait in the hall downstairs. They'll want to see you.'

'I just want to be alone with you—to look at your face. I want to touch it and kiss it, and then look at it again and again.'

'Is it—what you expected?' she asked nervously.

'Yes, it is,' he said in a tone of wonder. 'It's strange, but I seem always to have known how you would look.'

Her heart was thumping. At any moment he would recognise her. She must tell him now, without further delay.

'Jason, I—'

There was a knock on the door and Hilda's voice called, 'Can we come in?'

'I suppose it would be unkind to keep them out,' Jason said with a reluctant sigh. 'But soon you and I will be together and then—there's so much I want to say.'

The rest of the day was given over to celebrations.

Jason showed himself to his eager staff, then hauled himself on crutches to the stables, to see the horses. It was wonderful to watch him greeting old friends with love, stroking their noses, and at last seeing for himself that they were unhurt.

But every few moments he glanced across at Elinor, as if trying to reassure himself that she was still there. And she knew that for him, as for her, this was simply going through the motions until their moment should come.

At last he'd paid his dues to his household, and was free to admit that he was tiring.

'You've overdone it,' Elinor said. 'You were bound to, but it's time to have a rest.'

'Yes, Nurse,' he said with suspicious meekness.

Perhaps Hilda had guessed something, for they found champagne and two glasses waiting in his room. Elinor poured the sparkling liquid, and they drank a triumphant toast, smiling into each other's eyes.

Jason's face was pale from the exhausting day, but nothing could quench his joy. When she'd helped him onto the bed he pulled her down beside him and straight into his arms.

It was their first kiss as equals, the first kiss in which she could risk putting her whole heart. And she did so, nothing held back, telling him silently that he was now her whole life, and she was his however he wanted.

'Elinor,' he murmured. 'Elinor…'

Her name sounded sweet on his lips. He said it in a

special way, as though he was naming something sacred and precious. 'I didn't imagine last night, did I?' he whispered. 'It wasn't just a beautiful dream?'

'No, it wasn't a dream,' she said joyfully.

The past was forgotten. He wasn't the man she'd hated, he was the man she loved, would love until she died.

'Do I need to say it?' he whispered.

'No, my dearest. You don't have to, but—'

She wanted to hear the words of love, now that she was free at last to show her feelings. There were so many ways to love, and so many glorious years ahead to spend finding new ways. This was the moment she'd waited and longed for—for six years, although she hadn't known it—and she was going to savour it to the utmost.

'Jason,' she murmured.

'I love to hear you speak my name.'

She said it again and again, and Jason smiled in a happiness that echoed her own. He drew back and gazed down into her face with a look of adoration.

Then something seemed to strike him. He drew a sharp breath, and as she watched his smile faded, to be replaced by disbelief, then belief, then shock.

'You,' he breathed. *'You!'*

CHAPTER ELEVEN

JASON spoke slowly, as though unable to believe his own words.

'You're the girl Simon wanted to marry—he brought you here that summer—Cindy Smith.'

He drew back, letting his arms fall away from her. His face, which a moment before had been full of adoration, was cold and withdrawn.

'Cindy Smith,' he repeated. 'I don't believe it! And yet—'

Elinor's heart was thumping. She'd imagined this moment so often, but her worst fears had never warned her of the bleak, unforgiving look in his eyes. She stood up from the bed.

'Yes. Elinor Lucinda Smith, whom you once knew as Cindy.'

'My God!' he whispered, appalled. 'My God!'

Abruptly he thrust himself up off the bed, staggered and grasped the dressing table to steady himself. Elinor reached out for him but he fended her off. '*No!* Stay away from me. Stand back and let me look at you.'

She didn't move. She was watching him, waiting for his disbelieving anger to pass. It was natural that he should be upset, just at first. But in a moment he would calm down, and all would be well.

She waited, and waited. But his hard eyes showed no sign of relenting, and fear began to creep over her like a deadly cold.

'You said you'd come back for your revenge,' he said at last. 'And you did.'

'No,' she protested indignantly. 'I said I'd come back, but I never said it was for revenge.'

'Why else? What a wonderful chance for you. All this time, you've had me at your mercy, haven't you?'

'I haven't thought about that,' she said, very pale. 'You've been a patient, like any other.'

He made a sound of disbelief. Elinor began to take deep breaths to fight down the violent feelings that welled up in her. This was worse than anything she could have imagined. The love and understanding that had united them, and which she'd relied on for this moment, might never have been.

'I can remember you looking out of the train window, warning me that you'd be back one day, with more hate on your face than I've ever seen.'

'I had reason to hate you. You destroyed me because you thought I wasn't good enough for your family. But I said I was going to prove you wrong. *Then* I'd be back. I only wanted to make you admit that I was better than you gave me credit for.'

He was clinging to the wall for support, determined to confront this moment on his feet.

'Fine, if you'd been honest with me at the outset. But you didn't tell me who you were. All this time you've known the truth and I haven't. That's what I can't bear. It must have given you a good laugh.'

'I kept quiet for your sake.'

'Don't take me for a fool—' he raged.

'You had enough pressure without that. I did it to spare you even more.'

'I'm disappointed in you,' he said sarcastically. 'You had the guts to take your revenge, now have the guts to enjoy it openly. It was a damned good revenge, wasn't it? You made me believe you were the one person I could trust. I told you things I've never told another living soul. I even—' He stopped with a shudder. 'And all the time you were gloating.'

'How dare you?' she breathed. 'You know nothing about me. You didn't then and you don't now. I didn't want this job. I tried to turn it down, but someone backed out at the last minute. But for that I'd never have come within a mile of you.'

His face was ravaged. 'But somehow you forced yourself. I wonder why? It couldn't have been the chance to see me brought low, could it?' There was terrible bitterness in his voice.

'Can't you understand that I didn't want to see or think of you again?'

He turned away from her and hobbled painfully towards the window. He wanted to look outside, anywhere but at the face that had watched him when he was unaware. He thought of the nights she'd sat up with him, listening while he poured out his heart.

He'd always found it easier to act than talk, but in her sympathetic presence the words had flowed—words of longing and loneliness, of fear and vulnerability. And all the time…

He groaned aloud to think how he'd exposed his soul to this woman of all women.

He swung around to study her. Yes, it was really Cindy. And now he understood why he hadn't recognised her at once. What did this poised, defiant young woman have in common with the tearful girl he'd banished six years ago?

The eyes were the same, still large, blue and beautiful. But the mouth was different, its vulnerability less evident, its strength more pronounced. How had one woman become the other?

Then he recalled the gentle words that had fallen from that mouth, words that had reached out to him in his agony, and kept him from sinking into hell. He remembered other things too. Lips brushing his in the darkness, the enveloping warmth of compassion that had saved his sanity.

All based on deceit. He clenched his hands and the sweat stood out on his brow.

Elinor watched him, pervaded by sick horror. She was back in another time, with Simon judging her, hurling accusations, showing no mercy. How easily he'd assumed the worst then. How easily Jason assumed the worst now. She felt as if she was choking. They were both alike: hard, unforgiving, without understanding or pity.

But, even knowing that, nothing prepared her for the cruelty of his next words.

'I wonder how much you really wanted me to see again?' he asked sarcastically. 'I was going to ask you to marry me, but you guessed that, of course. If I'd stayed blind, you could have continued the deception. And that would have been the biggest laugh of all.

'And when I could see—I still didn't know you at first. I wonder when you were going to tell me—or should I say *if*?'

'I was—going to tell you—' she faltered. 'I was—'

She couldn't bear any more. Turning, she rushed out of the room, and was halfway down the corridor before she stopped, as though something had brought a hand down on her shoulder.

'No,' she said fiercely. 'Not this time. No more running away.'

She'd stumbled from the room with tears in her eyes.

She walked back with her head high and a heart that had turned to stone.

'How dare you speak to me like that?' she demanded furiously. 'Six years ago you accused me of scheming to marry your brother for his money. Now you accuse me of plotting to marry you. You're deluding yourself. No woman in her senses would want to marry a man with a hard, closed mind, a cruel, unforgiving bigot. Believe me, Jason, there's no money in the world could make it worth my while to marry you. You should be ashamed.'

He knew it. The flush on his cheeks told her that.

'I went too far,' he said curtly. 'I take back that last remark. But you can't stay here. It's better for both of us if you leave first thing tomorrow.'

'No.'

He stared. 'What did you say?'

'I won't go. You threw me out once before, and I scuttled away like the frightened little thing I was. But I'm not little or frightened now. I'm going to stay and finish my work.'

'The devil you are! One call from me to your agency—'

'They'll want to know why, Jason. What are you going to tell them? That I'm a bad nurse? You won't say that because it's not true, and you're not a liar.'

She didn't add that he couldn't tell them the real reason, but she saw in his face that he knew it. He glared at her bitterly.

'You think you're damned clever, don't you, *Nurse Smith*?'

'No, I think I'm here to do a job, and I'm going to do it. You can walk a bit, but not enough. When you're ready to face the world, then I'll have what I came back for. After that, you won't see me for dust.'

Her anger was growing by the minute.

'I can't believe you judged me so easily,' she went on.
'I've done everything I could to get you better, not just
being your nurse, but lying awake thinking of things that
would help you.

'I didn't want to come here. You were my enemy, but
I didn't hate you any more. I didn't feel anything.' Her
voice trembled and she added defiantly, 'I never do these
days. You were a job I was going to take care of as
quickly as possible, and then get out.

'But you needed me, and the patient's needs come first.
I didn't tell you I was Cindy because in the state you were
in then you couldn't have endured it. I wasn't gloating, I
was thinking of you. Once I'd made that decision I had
to stick with it. And frankly it didn't seem so important.'

'Look—'

'Be quiet. I'm talking now, and Jason Tenby is going
to listen for once in his life. I've done a good job with
you, and I deserved better than to have you turn on me.
I began to think you'd actually changed. Isn't that funny?
It seemed as though the intolerant, arrogant man I once
knew had learned kindness and understanding. But I was
wrong. You haven't learned a thing.'

In a gesture of defiance she seized her champagne glass,
and raised it in ironic salute.

'So here's to your speedy recovery and an early parting!
A relief to both of us. And for the rest of your life you'll
know that you owe it to a woman you despised. *That* will
be my revenge.'

'Some hell of a revenge!'

'Live with it!' she said bitterly, and drained the glass.

Without waiting for an answer she walked out: out of
his room, out of his house. If she could have walked out
of his life at that moment she would have done it. Pride
and anger raged through her. How naive of her to imagine

that Jason Tenby had softened! The hard inner core of the man was as proud and ruthless as ever.

But what did it matter? She couldn't be hurt because she felt nothing. She allowed herself to feel nothing. That was how it had been for six years, and now that was how it would always be. So she was safe. Nothing could ever touch her again. Nothing. *Nothing.*

Her resolve almost cracked when she saw Jason next day. He looked as if he'd spent the night pursued by furies. There were dark shadows under his eyes, and his mouth had the tension she'd seen when she'd first come here, but which had been banished recently. She looked away, refusing to see it.

He regarded her warily as she entered his room, once more wearing her nurse's uniform. But although he grimaced he didn't refer to it.

'I apologise for what I said last night,' he said at once.

'It doesn't matter. You'd had a shock and it was just reaction. There's no need to mention it again.'

'But I want to mention it. You were right in all you said. I was ungrateful dog to turn on you like that. And I'm sorry.'

'It's perfectly all right.'

'Dammit, stop talking to me like that!' he grated. 'Every word you say is coming out of the nurse's handbook: Never take offence if the patient acts like a jerk. Make allowances for him, and above all don't treat him as an equal.'

'Well, we're not equals. We're patient and nurse and we should never have forgotten it. Your recovery is all that counts. I have no feelings in the matter.'

'Is that really true, Elinor? Did I only imagine that we—?'

'I think we should discuss your treatment, Mr Tenby. We still have a lot of work to do.'

With a sinking heart Jason recognised the voice he'd heard when she'd first come here: efficient, cool, dead. And now he saw that her eyes too were remote, as though it was only by banishing life to a distant place that she could bear to exist. Right in front of him she was deliberately turning herself back into an automaton.

'Elinor,' he said. 'Please, listen—'

'You rather overdid things yesterday,' the automaton said. 'I suggest you take it a little easier today.'

'Very well,' he said, giving up for the moment.

'I have some notes to make. I'll see you after breakfast.'

They usually ate together, but for now he had no choice but to do things her way. He breakfasted off bitterness and dismay, and a kind of horror at what he could see happening to her.

She looked pale and strained, and he wondered if her night had been as bad as his own. Worse, if her face told the true story.

He could have cut his tongue out. He'd spoken in a state of shock, and regretted it almost at once. In the small hours of the night he'd asked himself how he would have felt if she'd disclosed her identity at the start, and he knew it would only have added to his torment. And once the innocent deception had begun she'd had to go on with it.

Today should have been the happiest of his life. But in the midst of joy he had an intolerable sense of loss. He knew he was to blame, but the woman he'd come to know over the last few weeks would never have reacted in this cold, unforgiving way.

He seemed to have lost Elinor completely. In her place

was a stranger. Neither Elinor nor Cindy. The pain of it
was like grieving for a death.

Somehow a routine established itself. A day passed into
a week, and then into two weeks. He grew stronger, his
walking more assured.

But the old, sweet companionship was gone. Elinor
wore her uniform, called him Mr Tenby, and never spent
a moment more in his company than her work demanded.
He was unhappy, but he could have borne that. It was her
unhappiness that tormented him.

He could see her getting thinner, the dark shadows ap-
pearing under her eyes. He wasn't a subtle man where
people were concerned, but his love gave him insight and
he could tell that there was more troubling her than simply
a quarrel. It was as though she'd had a blow over the
heart, and it had drained the spirit out of her.

He would have given anything to undo what he'd done.
But he didn't know how, and she either couldn't or
wouldn't tell him. The time was slipping remorselessly
past, and if he didn't find the answer soon he would lose
her for ever.

Several times he insisted that they go riding. They always paused at the same place by the stream, because the
tree stump made it easy for him to dismount. She would
help him down then stand away quickly, but once he
pulled her close before she could back off, and forced his
kiss on her.

It was rough and uncivilised, but he was getting desperate.

'No—' she tried to protest.

He ignored her, kissing her with fierce, possessive urgency. Elinor knew this was dangerous. She'd thought
hard about Jason, and decided against him. But her body

knew nothing of her thoughts, or at least disagreed with them. It persisted in responding to him.

She put out all her strength to resist, but there was no escape from his passion, from her own, from the thundering of her heart.

'I want to know that this was real,' he said against her mouth. 'What we had—it wasn't my imagination.'

'What we had is over,' she gasped.

His answer was to cover her mouth again. His lips were warm and firm, reminding her of how desire felt with the man she loved, would always love. She could have cried out at the torment of having to leave him when her heart yearned towards him. But her decision was made. She wouldn't give in to weakness. She couldn't afford to.

'Let me go, Jason. Let me go *now*.'

Something in her voice warned him of danger. He slackened his hold, but still kept one arm about her.

'Elinor, don't do this,' he begged. 'When two people share what we do, you can't just pretend it didn't exist.'

She didn't answer, but looked at him with a face full of such suffering that he drew in his breath.

'I thought you loved me,' he said. 'Was it all an illusion? Were you only sorry for your patient?'

She shook her head, unable to speak for the strength of her emotion.

'Then we have to talk,' he said.

He sat down on the stump. Elinor tied up the horses and sat too, but not close to him. Although it was a warm day she was shivering. Jason longed to reach out and enfold her in his arms, but instinct told him that if he touched her now she would run away and vanish for ever.

'We've got to talk,' he repeated. 'I love you, Elinor.'

'*Please*, Jason—' she cried as though the words hurt her.

'Listen to me. If Virginia hadn't broken off our engagement, I was going to do it myself. I meant to tell you that before, but other things got in the way. It's you I want to marry.'

She gave a hard laugh. 'Once you thought I wasn't good enough to marry a Tenby—'

'To hell with that! My family are a load of jumped up hucksters who struck lucky. None of them have had your generosity and compassion. We'll be a better family when you're one of us.'

'*No!*' she cried. 'It's too late.'

'Look at me.' He reached for her but she jumped up quickly and moved away.

'Don't go away from me, darling,' he begged. 'I can't follow you.'

But she stayed at a distance, leaning against the tree, looking at him out of burning, reproachful eyes. He could see she was at the end of her tether, and it hurt him to push her further, but this was a chance that might never come again.

He spoke carefully. 'You told me once about the man who left you with a maimed life. It was Simon, wasn't it? Don't tell me you're still in love with him?'

Elinor shook her head without speaking.

'Then what made you retreat into that "safe place"?'

'You did,' she said simply. 'Years ago when you made Simon dump me.'

'But I didn't break your engagement because you "weren't good enough" for Simon. I did it because you were *too* good for him.

'I'd seen the lives he'd ruined, the girls whose hearts he'd broken. Simon is charming on the surface, but underneath he's cruel, cold and spiteful. Even to you. Do you remember our very first meeting in the factory, when you were a child?'

'Yes, and you recognised me and threw it at me when we met again.'

'Elinor, I never recognised you. Simon told me an hour after I met you.'

'But he promised not to tell,' she cried.

'Betraying people's awkward little secrets is his idea of a laugh. I'm told he makes love charmingly, but inside there's nothing but cold selfishness. You were so sweet and young and innocent. I had to protect you.

'Words were useless. You wouldn't have believed me. So I tried to scare you off, offered you money. Nothing worked. But then I discovered that some nasty characters were putting pressure on him about gambling debts that he couldn't pay. I told him he wouldn't get a penny from me until he sent you away.

'He made me a fine speech about not being "bullied out of his love", but, believe me, after that he was looking for an excuse to put the blame on you. When I kissed you that night it was an act of desperation. I knew he'd see us, and it gave him the excuse he needed. After that I had to make you leave quickly, because when we kissed—I never expected what happened. Do you remember?'

'Yes, I remember,' she said in a low voice.

'No woman had ever affected me like that. But you were little more than a child. And you were in love with Simon, however mistakenly. How could I—? I was afraid of myself, of how I might behave.

'I thought you'd find someone else in no time. But I'd never heard anyone cry as you did, and I knew then that something had gone horribly wrong. After you left I had no peace of mind.

'So I tried to find you again. I was haunted by the sound

of your weeping. I searched for months but I couldn't find you. Everything was confused. It's been confused ever since.'

He waited to see if she would say anything, but she only stared at the grass.

'I changed after that,' he went on. 'I started to see how my actions felt to other people. I owed that to you as I owe everything else to you. And now, surely—'

'Now? There is no now, can't you understand that?'

'Look me in the eye and tell me that you don't love me.'

She shook her head.

'Then why? Because I lost my temper unreasonably? I acted like a swine but can't you forgive? People who love each other do forgive.'

'Normal people, yes. But there's something in me that can't. It isn't lack of forgiveness. It's fear. I can't take the risks of love any more.'

'Then what?' he said angrily. 'Go back into that safe place? For ever?'

'Yes, if I want to.'

'Do you know what you're condemning yourself to?'

'That's my choice,' she said desperately. 'Leave me alone, Jason. I won't let you hurt me again. I *can't*.'

He stared at her, aghast at her misery. At that moment he would have done anything, made any sacrifice, to end her suffering.

'My poor darling,' he said softly.

'Don't call me that!' she cried. 'I'm not yours. I'll never be yours however much I—not now. It's too late.'

She stood up straight from the tree and went to the horses. She started untying Tansy, but suddenly the strength seemed to go out of her, and she leaned against the mare's neck, her face averted, her shoulders shaking.

Jason watched her, and a look of anguish came into his eyes.

'Dear God!' he whispered. 'What have I done?'

Elinor happened to be present when the factory manager said, 'We should be having the firm's annual dinner dance in three weeks. Do you want me to cancel it?'

'Certainly not,' Jason replied.

'And you can tell them Mr Tenby will be there,' Elinor put in. 'On his feet.'

They looked at each other. Elinor gave a nod so slight that only he could see it.

'You sound very sure,' Jason said when they were alone.

'I'm sure,' she said quietly.

'Only if you're there too.'

'I wouldn't miss it for anything.'

'Oh, yes,' he said wryly. 'Your revenge.'

Once this was to have been a sweet time for them. He would have practised his dancing skills, holding onto her, and they would have laughed and kissed. Now Elinor worked hard on his legs, gave him exercises to practise, and bid him goodnight. He longed to reach out to her, but after the last time he was too afraid of hurting her.

When the evening came she wore the special dress he'd bought her.

'You look glorious,' he said sincerely.

'I mean to do you credit.'

He was startlingly handsome in the black dinner jacket he'd worn on the evening of their dinner. Together they made a splendid pair as they walked downstairs, with Jason using only a walking stick for support.

Alf drove them into Hampton Tenby. The firm had hired the town hall for the occasion, and they arrived to find the place glittering. Lights poured out onto the pavement. They were the last to arrive, and everyone was eagerly awaiting them.

'Shall I get the stick?' she asked.

'No,' he said. 'Not this time.'

'Do you think you're ready to do it alone?'

'Not alone. With you.'

It was like a trumpet call to action. She turned and looked at him with blazing eyes. 'Right,' she said.

Between them they managed it smoothly, guided by their instinctive understanding, which worked perfectly even now. Jason got out and stood, looking casual but actually supporting himself against the car, while Elinor came around to him. It was the most natural thing in the world for him to slip his arm through hers, and only she knew how much he was leaning on her.

'Ready?' she asked quietly.

'Ready.'

Together they moved forward, one step, then another. Through the contact of their bodies she could feel him growing more confident every moment.

A cheering broke out as they walked through the main door into the building. Every man and woman who worked in the factory was there to see Jason Tenby come back to them.

The manager shook Jason's hand, and Elinor's. Then Jason indicated her for the crowd's acclaim, sweeping one arm around the circle of his employees, and keeping the other across her shoulders, leaning on her slightly.

As they entered the ballroom the band played 'Hail The Conquering Hero Comes'. It was corny but it was also heartfelt. The smiles and applause told Elinor that. For the first time she understood just how popular Jason was with his employees.

She regarded him, walking with his head held high, carried at the familiar proud angle. But the next moment she wished she hadn't looked, because he turned to meet her eyes, and her heart skipped a beat.

She didn't want to be reminded how she felt about him in case it undermined her resolve to leave. But she would conquer that, she promised herself. This was the night she'd waited for. After this she could leave and seek refuge in the safe place, where there was no pain because there was no anything.

But her heart still prompted her to steal glances at him, storing up exactly the memories she wanted to forget.

How could she ever forget climbing together onto the raised dais where the top table stood, festooned with flowers? Or the way he handed her to the place of honour beside him, pulling out her chair, refusing to sit until she did, and making it clear to everyone that she was special?

As they ate a stream of people stopped at their table to shake Jason's hand, so many that he hardly managed to eat anything. After the meal came the speeches and the toasts.

Jason rose to his feet and stood straight and upright, showing himself to them while they cheered him to the echo.

The lion had returned in triumph.

They listened, hushed, as he began to speak.

'Most of you don't know the lady sitting beside me,' he said, 'but it's time you did, because without her I wouldn't be here. Her title is Nurse Elinor Smith, but I call her Dragon Lady, because she's had to be a dragon to bully me back to health.'

Everyone laughed, as they were meant to. Jason went on. 'I was the worst patient in the world, but she survived me, and showed me how to survive.'

He gave a light, half-humorous account of the past weeks, and what he owed her. This was Jason at his best—confident, witty and generous. Elinor listened with a lump in her throat. This was something she wouldn't even try to forget.

At last he raised his champagne glass.

'I ask you all to drink with me to the finest nurse in the world,' he said simply.

Everybody stood, raised their glasses and toasted her. Elinor covered her eyes but Jason took her hand away and kissed it. She looked up but she could hardly see him through the blur of her tears.

To her relief he didn't ask her to respond, and the rest of the speeches flowed on over her. Under cover of the hum he leaned to her and whispered, 'I didn't do wrong, did I?'

'No, it was very nice of you,' she said huskily.

The speeches came to an end and the floor was cleared for dancing. Jason held out his hand.

'You promised me,' he reminded her, 'that one day we would dance together.'

He led her down onto the floor and as if dreaming she went into his arms. This would be a memory to treasure in the lonely years ahead; the closeness of his body to hers, the way they moved together, the ardour in his eyes.

He danced stiffly, still relying on her for support.

But he could dance.

'See how I still need you,' he murmured. 'As I always will.'

'Not any more,' she sighed. 'Oh, Jason, you shouldn't have done this.'

'Isn't revenge so sweet after all?'

'You know I didn't mean that. This isn't revenge to me, it's—a kind of torture.'

'No worse than we'll both endure for years to come. This is what I want you to remember—how we danced together, and I told you that I loved you, and you threw it all away for the sake of your pride.'

'It isn't pride, Jason. Please believe that. It's fear. I guess I'm not as strong as I thought I was.'

'Love is supposed to cast out fear,' he reminded her, 'but only if the love is strong enough. And if you don't love me enough for that—' his face darkened almost into despair '—then I have only myself to blame.'

Tears stung her eyes as the music swelled around them, and they danced to the smiles and applause of Jason's colleagues.

This was her moment of triumph, and it was very bitter.

Jason, watching her face closely, understood her. He knew her so well now that not a thought could pass across her face without his reading it. She was as far away from him as ever.

He began to feel desperate. He'd tried everything and there seemed nothing left.

The dance ended. His legs were aching and he needed to think, but his manager's wife cornered him and began to talk about horses. He answered mechanically.

'Yes, beautiful animals—lucky that every one was saved—went to the stables and felt them for myself—wonderful moment—'

Abruptly he stopped talking and drew in a sharp breath. Illumination flooded his face.

'That's it!' he murmured to himself. 'What a fool I've been. What a blind, stupid fool!'

CHAPTER TWELVE

ELINOR agreed to stay an extra couple of days for Andrew's final visit.

'He'll want to talk to you,' Jason said. 'Your knowledge of the case is more up-to-date than his.'

He spoke coolly and with a lack of emotion that made it possible for her to agree. It was obvious that Jason had finally accepted her decision, for which she told herself to be glad. She passed the time out of doors, using Bob as an excuse.

'Not again,' she told him at last when he dropped the ball at her feet for the hundredth time. 'Time we went back.'

As she approached the house she saw an unfamiliar vehicle outside the door. It was brand-new and a very expensive make, the car of a man who'd done well in the world.

Probably a business contact of Jason's, she thought.

She entered the house quietly, hoping to get upstairs without being seen.

But then she checked, brought up short by the sound of a voice that had once made her heart beat madly.

'And the next thing I knew they'd agreed to my terms—of course I always knew they would—'

'Simon,' she whispered.

Next came the sound of his laughter. He was in the study, the door to which stood open. Elinor paused, trying to find the will-power to move. She ought to climb the stairs, but the temptation to go back and see him was almost overpowering.

While she was still debating, Jason's voice called out, 'Come in, Elinor.'

At first she had only a confused impression of the scene. There was Jason, his eyes turned to the door, regarding her intently. And there was a younger man, just turning around.

He was heavier, and the sheen of good living was on him. His hair, once attractively unkempt, had been cut and shaped by an expert. His clothes, his gold watch spoke of money.

As he advanced across the floor his smile was full of a slightly self-conscious charm. 'How do you do?' he said, taking her hand in both of his. 'So you're the angel of mercy who's saved Jason.'

'I'm Jason's nurse, yes,' she said uncertainly.

'It's meant so much to know he was in good hands. We've all been so worried about him.'

Not worried enough to visit him recently, she thought.

She wanted to flinch away. There was something unpleasant about this sleek young man. His expensive attire couldn't disguise the fact that he was going to seed through self-indulgence. Seedy. Yes, that was it. Expensive, pampered, and seedy.

Something seemed to strike him. He searched her face. 'Are you—? Have we met before?'

'Six years ago,' she said in a voice whose calmness surprised herself.

'That's right,' he said softly. 'Cindy. Little Cindy Smith. Well, by all that's wonderful. Come here!'

He put his arms around her and the smell of his aftershave nearly overpowered her. She managed to avert her face and his kiss fell on her cheek. He released her and held her away from him.

'Cindy! My little Cindy!'

'I'm not "little Cindy" any more. Not for six years.'

His eyes flickered uncertainly, as if he suspected a double meaning. Elinor was intensely aware of Jason watching them.

'Come and meet my wife,' Simon said, half turning to the woman behind him. 'Darling, this is Jason's saviour.'

Simon's wife came as a shock. Jason had said she was a little older than him, but Elinor would have estimated the gap as at least ten years.

She was fair, and pretty, but her face had a permanently anxious look. Like Simon she was expensively dressed, but with far more taste. She greeted Elinor with gentle charm.

'It's really wonderful what you've done for Jason,' she said softly. 'He says you helped him more than anybody else could have done.' The words were said with a grave simplicity that touched Elinor as Simon's effusions had failed to do.

When she turned to leave Jason limped after her, using his stick. 'I hope you'll join us for dinner.'

'Don't you want to be alone with your family?'

His eyes met hers. 'You know better than that.'

'You sent for them, didn't you?'

'Yes. I wanted you to see him for yourself.'

'What are you playing at, Jason?'

'I was never in greater earnest in my life.'

It felt eerie to be sitting down to dinner again with Simon and Jason. She'd been on edge then and she was on edge now, but for a different reason. Simon did most of the talking. Carole spoke rarely, and always with a quick glance at her husband first.

She's afraid of him, Elinor thought, with shock. How could anybody be afraid of Simon?

But this wasn't the delightful boy she'd known. This was a sleek, hard man with a slippery surface. Again she heard Jason saying, 'Underneath he's cruel—cold and spiteful.'

Simon talked on, pronouncing ignorantly on one subject after another. An eighteen-year-old girl, blinded by love, hadn't noticed that he was shallow and stupid. But she wasn't eighteen any more, and this pompous, self-satisfied man—she nearly thought 'little man'—was getting on her nerves.

When the meal was over she excused herself quickly. She headed upstairs, but when she was halfway up she heard her name called in a laughing voice, and Simon bounded up to join her on the landing.

'I've been longing to get you alone all evening,' he said. 'Oh, Cindy, what a smasher you turned out to be!'

'My name is Elinor,' she said.

'To me you'll always be my sweet Cindy.'

'That's not what you called me last time we met,' she reminded him. 'No word was bad enough for me then.'

He smiled. 'That's long ago. Why rake up the past?'

'It was money, wasn't it? Jason threatened to turn off the supply if you didn't dump me. You seized the excuse.'

'Well, a man needs money to live.'

'Then why ask me to marry you at all? You knew I was poor.'

'But being in love with you was so much fun. I simply adored you. You'll never know how much.'

'Oh, I think I know exactly how much,' Elinor said evenly.

He missed her irony. 'I thought Jason would be so pleased to see me settle down that he'd cough up. But he turned awkward. Anyway, who cares about that now?'

'Yes, I think we should forget it now that you're married.'

He chuckled. 'Carole's a sweetie, isn't she? And rolling in filthy lucre.'

'Otherwise, of course, you wouldn't have married her?'

'Carole and I understand each other. Mind you, she gets a bit difficult now and then. It's not the same as having your own cash. Between you and me, sweetie, it's a pity you nursed Jason quite so brilliantly. Know what I mean?'

'Yes, I know what you mean,' Elinor said, almost unable to speak through her disgust.

'Still, too late now. Come here, and give me a kiss for old time's sake.'

'If,' Elinor said, speaking distinctly, 'you dare to lay a finger on me, I shall slap your face so hard that the mark will show for a week. And then Carole might stop your pocket money.'

His smile faded. Before her eyes he turned into the man he really was, the man Jason had tried to warn her about.

'Bitch!' he spat.

'As long as we understand each other.'

Andrew called early next morning, pronounced Jason fit, and congratulated her. Elinor thanked him and went to finish her packing. She had nearly finished when she heard Andrew's car drive away.

She went looking for a book she thought she'd left downstairs. But as she crossed the hall she heard Carole's voice coming from inside the conservatory. She started to back away, but something in the other woman's voice held her. Carole sounded as if she was talking through tears.

'It wouldn't matter so much if you didn't lie about it.'

Then Simon, bored and irritated. 'I didn't lie.'

'You said you didn't know her—but you did, didn't you?'

'Years ago; it was nothing.'

'You were in love with her.'

'Good lord, no! She set her cap at me, but she never meant a thing to me.'

'I don't believe you,' Carole cried passionately. 'You called her "little Cindy". Why do you call her Cindy if her name's Elinor?'

'All right, all right, it was a pet name. So what? Do I have to make a grand confession of every little thing that happened to me in the past? I tell you, Carole, if you don't stop making my life a misery with your jealousy, I really will find another woman, and it'll be all your own fault.'

There was the sound of desperate sobbing.

'Here we go!' Simon sneered. 'The waterworks again.'

'Why do you talk to me like that?' Carole sobbed. 'Oh, darling, we used to be so happy. You said you loved me. What went wrong?'

'Hey, come on!' To Elinor's relief Simon's voice was gentler. 'Don't be a silly girl. You know I don't care for anyone but you.'

Elinor leaned against the wall. She hadn't meant to eavesdrop but she was so horrified by what she'd heard that she couldn't tear herself away. Simon had already shocked her with his crude wish for Jason's death, but this was almost as bad.

Carole said something she couldn't catch, then Simon replied, 'We're not going to quarrel about money, are we? So I overdrew a little—all right, I overdrew a lot, but what the hell? There's plenty where that comes from. Write me a cheque, there's a good girl! And finish the packing. I want to get out of here pronto.'

'Today? But you know how I like staying here—'

'Well, we can't. I've got to meet a man in London this afternoon. So hurry up.'

Elinor backed quickly as she heard his footsteps heading for the door. Simon emerged and went upstairs without seeing her. From inside the room came the sound of heartbroken weeping.

If she'd cherished any lingering belief in him, it was gone. Simon, the greedy, cold-blooded bully, swearing he loved her but betraying her pathetic little secret to Jason 'for a good laugh.' Simon, sneering at his wife while throwing her money away.

'Do you understand now?'

Jason had been standing in the shadows, watching her. He took her arm and drew her into the library.

'He married Carole for her money,' he said, 'and he doesn't even treat her decently. It could have been you, crying your heart out.'

'Yes, I see that,' she said. 'But there was no need for this, Jason. I believed you.'

'Only with your head. Like me with the horses. I didn't really believe they were safe until you took me to the stables to feel them. There's no substitute for your own experience.' He gave her a wry smile. 'Another thing I owe to you.'

Carole appeared in the doorway. She'd dried her tears and now wore a bright, forced smile.

'It's been a lovely visit, but we have to be going,' she said huskily. 'I've got an appointment in London today—I'd forgotten.'

Jason spoke to her kindly and led her away with his arm around her shoulders.

Elinor let out her breath. She felt desperately sorry for Simon's wife, and deeply thankful that it wasn't herself.

She knew that in bringing Simon here Jason had done something valuable for her. A weight seemed to have gone from her shoulders. For six years she'd suffered the trauma of that night, and her subconscious feeling of guilt at responding to Jason's kisses.

Now she knew herself to be innocent. She could leave this place with an easy mind, and somehow, somewhere, she would find the strength to start her life again.

Jason returned, closed the door behind him and stood looking at her.

'You were right about Simon,' she told him. 'It was all there, but I was too young and blind to see it.'

'But you've seen it now. So can't we—?'

'Jason, I'm going away—' she said quickly.

'Then I was wrong,' he said, moving close and looking intently into her eyes. 'You can't forgive me?'

'There's nothing to forgive—not any more. But too much has happened. How can we—you and I of all people—ever find peace together?'

'It wasn't peace I had in mind,' he said, with a flash of something in his eyes that made a blush start in her. 'Not just at first, anyway. Peace is for the old, and when we've grown old together we'll worry about peace. Whether we'll find it, I don't know. But I do know that neither of us can ever find it with anyone else.'

'There'll never be anyone else for me,' she agreed. 'But don't press me on this, Jason. Please.'

'You're really going?' he whispered.

She nodded and his face became bleak.

'Then I'll drive you to the station,' he said. 'There's an irony in that that I'm sure we'll both appreciate.'

She'd tried not to let herself think as the countryside sped past the car. Last time had been terrible, but this time was worse. She would blank out all thought and emotion until she was well away.

Even now she watched him anxiously as he limped up the steps to the platform, with the aid of his walking stick. The train came trundling in slowly. He pulled open the door, and thrust her bag inside. She got in and looked at him through the open window as she had done long ago.

'We've a moment yet,' he said. 'It's not too late to change your mind.'

'It's been too late for a long time,' she said sadly. 'Goodbye, my darling. Don't hate me for being a coward. Try to understand that I'm doing what I must.'

'I could never hate you. Only myself. If you can't take the love I offer, then I damaged you beyond repair. I've killed love in the only woman whose love I want, and I'll live with that guilt all my life. But one day—Elinor—surely—?'

'One day is so far away,' she said in anguish. She took his face between her hands and covered it with kisses.

'Goodbye, my love,' she whispered through her tears. 'Goodbye—goodbye—'

The guard blew his whistle. The train began to move.

She touched his face gently one last time, and then they were apart. The distance between them was growing, slowly but inexorably.

'Elinor,' he called. *'Elinor!'*

Suddenly, as if a curtain had parted, she saw what she was doing: condemning not only herself but him, whom she loved. She'd healed and protected him, and now she was abandoning him.

Love was stronger than fear. He'd said that and she knew it was true. The train was gathering speed. It had almost left the station. At the very last minute she threw open the door and jumped out, landing on her hands and knees. Someone in the train pulled the door shut again. She didn't see. She saw only the man standing at the far end of the platform, transfixed. He was the man she loved more than herself, more than her life. But she hadn't understood until it was almost too late.

'Jason!' she cried, trying to tell him everything in one desperate word.

She began to run to him. At the same moment he threw away his stick and took the first halting steps towards her. Then more steps, and more, growing in strength and confidence as he realised the glorious truth.

And then he too was running, his arms outstretched to reach her, engulf her, hold her against his heart for ever.

COMING NEXT MONTH

MILLS & BOON®

Enchanted™

THE OUTBACK AFFAIR by Elizabeth Duke

Natasha was horrified when her tour guide turned out to be Tom Scanlon—the man who'd once jilted her. It was too intimate a situation for ex-lovers—but Tom wanted Natasha back. And now he had two weeks alone with her to prove just how much!

THE BEST MAN AND THE BRIDESMAID
by Liz Fielding

As chief bridesmaid, Daisy is forced out of her usual shapeless garb and into a beautiful dress. Suddenly the best man, determinedly single Robert Furneval, whom she has always loved, begins to see her in a whole new light…

HUSBAND ON DEMAND by Leigh Michaels

Jake Abbott has arrived at his brother's house—to discover that Cassie has been hired to look after the residence. He's clearly very happy for their temporary living arrangements to become more intimate. But what about permanent…?

THE FEISTY FIANCÉE by Jessica Steele

When Yanice fell for her boss, Thomson Wakefield, she adhered to her belief that love means marriage, but did it mean the same for him? A near tragic accident brings her answer, but can Yanice trust the proposal of a man under heavy sedation?

Available from 3rd March 2000

Three single women, one home-help agency—and three professional bachelors in search of...a wife?

✰ Are you a busy executive with a demanding career?

✰ Do you need help with those time-consuming everyday errands?

✰ Ever wished you could hire a house-sitter, caterer...or even a glamorous partner for that special social occasion?

*Meet **Cassie**, **Sabrina** and **Paige**—three independent women who've formed a business taking care of those troublesome domestic crises.*

And meet the three gorgeous bachelors who are simply looking for a little help...and instead discover they've hired Ms Right!

Enjoy bestselling author **Leigh Michaels's** new trilogy:

HUSBAND ON DEMAND—March 2000
BRIDE ON LOAN—May 2000
WIFE ON APPROVAL—July 2000

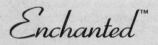

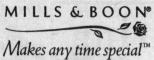

FREE!
2 Books
and a surprise gift!

We would like to take this opportunity to thank you for reading this Mills & Boon® book by offering you the chance to take TWO more specially selected titles from the Enchanted™ series absolutely FREE! We're also making this offer to introduce you to the benefits of the Reader Service™—

- ★ FREE home delivery
- ★ FREE gifts and competitions
- ★ FREE monthly Newsletter
- ★ Books available before they're in the shops
- ★ Exclusive Reader Service discounts

Accepting these FREE books and gift places you under no obligation to buy; you may cancel at any time, even after receiving your free shipment. Simply complete your details below and return the entire page to the address below. *You don't even need a stamp!*

YES! Please send me 2 free Enchanted books and a surprise gift. I understand that unless you hear from me, I will receive 4 superb new titles every month for just £2.40 each, postage and packing free. I am under no obligation to purchase any books and may cancel my subscription at any time. The free books and gift will be mine to keep in any case.

NOEB

Ms/Mrs/Miss/Mr ....Initials...
BLOCK CAPITALS PLEASE

Surname...

Address...

....

....Postcode ....

Send this whole page to:
UK: The Reader Service, FREEPOST CN81, Croydon, CR9 3WZ
EIRE: The Reader Service, PO Box 4546, Kilcock, County Kildare (stamp required)